RICARDA HUCH

*TRANSLATED FROM THE
GERMAN BY JAMIE BULLOCH*

Peirene

Der letzte Sommer

AUTHOR

Ricarda Huch (1864–1947) was a groundbreaking German historian, novelist and philosopher. As one of the first women to study at the University of Zurich, she received her doctorate in Philosophy and History in 1892. She authored numerous works on European history. She also wrote novels, poems and a play. *Der letzte Sommer* (*The Last Summer*) was first published in 1910. In 1926 she became the first female writer to be admitted to the Prussian Academy of Arts. She won from Thomas Mann the title 'The First Lady of Germany' – and even had an asteroid named in her honour.

TRANSLATOR

Jamie Bulloch is a historian, and has worked as a professional translator from German since 2001. His translations include books by Paulus Hochgatterer, Alissa Walser and Timur Vermes. Jamie is the translator of four previous Peirene titles: *Portrait of the Mother as a Young Woman* by Friedrich Christian Delius, *Sea of Ink* by Richard Weihe, *The Mussel Feast* by Birgit Vanderbeke and *The Empress and the Cake* by Linda Stift. Jamie won the 2014 Schlegel-Tieck Prize for Best German Translation for *The Mussel Feast*. He is also the author of *Karl Renner: Austria*.

MEIKE ZIERVOGEL
PEIRENE PRESS

I came upon this novel in the original German two years ago. And I loved it. It's a proper epistolary novel. Even though written more than 100 years ago, it feels as relevant now as then. *The Last Summer* asks how people can be trapped by an ideology. A topical story. An enjoyable read. A gem.

First published in Great Britain in 2017 by
Peirene Press Ltd
17 Cheverton Road
London N19 3BB
www.peirenepress.com

First published under the original German-language title *Der letzte Sommer*
Copyright © Insel Verlag 1950

All rights reserved by and controlled through Insel Verlag Anton Kippenberg
Berlin

This translation © Jamie Bulloch, 2017

ISBN 978-1-908670-34-2

Designed by Sacha Davison Lunt
Photographic image by Yury Kosourov / 123RF Stock Photo
Typeset by Tetragon, London
Printed and bound by T J International, Padstow, Cornwall

RICARDA HUCH

TRANSLATED FROM THE GERMAN BY JAMIE BULLOCH

Peirene

The Last Summer

Kremskoye, 5th May 19—

Dear Konstantin,

Having taken up my post, I will outline the situation as I find it here. I do not doubt that my plan will succeed; indeed, the circumstances appear even more favourable than might have been expected. The whole family seems well disposed towards me and I detect no hint of any suspicion, which is entirely natural, as only we in the know could fear the contrary. If the governor has made enquiries into my person, this cannot have done any harm, as all the way from elementary school to university my reports have been outstanding. The one thing that might paint me in a damaging light – my quarrel with my father – is mitigated by the fact that his domineering and eccentric personality is widely known. But I rather think that he has not undertaken such enquiries; the man is so completely free of mistrust that in his position his behaviour would be verging on naivety if it were not more a reflection of his fearlessness and his poor judgement of people. Besides, my

7

appointment seems to be entirely his wife's doing. An anxious woman by nature, ever since she received the threatening letter she thinks only of how she can protect her husband's life. Mistrust is not a feature of her character either; whilst she senses implausible dangers lurking at every turn, she would offer the murderer a spoonful of soup if she felt the poor man's belly were crying out for a drop of something warm.

She told me that the letter you wrote gave her the idea of seeking a young man who, under the pretext of working as her husband's secretary, would protect him from possible attacks without his realizing it. She had failed, however, to keep her fears or her plan secret from her husband. Eventually he gave in to her incessant pleading for the sake of peace, but also because he has been suffering recently from a type of neuralgia in his right arm, which is making writing difficult. His one stipulation was that – at night-time at least – he should be under the sole protection of his wife. The two of them laughed and he added that his wife was such a dab hand at making the bedroom secure that he could confidently place his trust in her. She never went to bed without first checking every single cupboard and especially the curtains, all of which she regarded as potential hiding places for criminals. Of course, she said spiritedly, one had to be circumspect, but she certainly wasn't afraid; why, she even left the windows open at night because she liked the fresh air. She was, however, toying with the idea of having bars fixed in front of them. For seeing as all the doors to the house were locked, those people with malicious intent would have no choice but to climb in through the window. Still, she did concede that she feels less apprehensive now that I am here. As she uttered these words there was something tremendously endearing about her expression. I said, 'I do hope so. Any worries you might have now I would deem an affront to my professional pride.' During our conversation their son came into the room. He gave me a look of concern and said, 'Are you starting today already?' This made us all laugh so much that it lightened the atmosphere at once. The son, his name is Velya, is a handsome and terribly droll young chap, not much younger than I, but he still behaves as a child of five, albeit with a slightly different set of toys. He is studying law in the hope of one day pursuing a diplomatic career, although you would not suppose any of this. Velya is a smart, modern individual with numerous unrestrained impulses. His susceptibility knows no bounds. All one can say about his character is that he has none, and this makes him thoroughly inconsequential. Things only interest him in so far as he can adorn them with his witticisms, the great and irresistible charm of which lies in the languid way he utters them.

Besides the son there are two daughters, Jessika and Katya, between twenty and twenty-three. Both are sweet, blonde creatures, so similar they could be twins. Initially they were prejudiced against me because they consider their mother's fear to be foolish and they were concerned that their summer seclusion might be disturbed. But as they find me handsome and stylish, and Velya, who is their role model, feels drawn to me, they're gradually coming round to the idea of my being here. I don't know why, but these three children remind me of little canaries huddled close together on their perch, chirruping away. There is something childishly harmless about the family overall, which could make me and my mission appear ridiculous to my eyes, but I'm sufficiently acquainted with the human soul to know that at its foundation is bottomless pride. Hatred, even ill-will assumes a certain familiarity with these people; deep down they feel themselves to be alone in a world that belongs to them. None of the others here are of particular significance and do not encroach upon their peace. The servants consist of a coachman, Ivan, who likes to drink – Velya calls him 'the gaffer' – and three maids. All of them are old-school Russians: they still feel like serfs, worship their masters and yet pass judgement on them with an unwitting sense of superiority because they are closer to the primary source of life. Dear creatures who, like animals, fill me with a certain awe.

Such are my initial impressions. You'll be hearing more from me soon.

Lyu

VELYA TO PETER

Kremskoye, 6th May

Dear Peter,

I've reconciled myself to having to stay here in the country for the entire duration of Papa's leave. This closing of the university is a very silly affair. I was surely right when I advocated a calm response, for it was predictable that in any struggle we'd come off second best. But of course there was no stopping you; you just had to dive in head first, and it's pure chance that you're not being sent to the gallows by my own father. There is absolutely no shame in submitting to a superior authority; on the contrary, trying to fight it is sheer stupidity, raving madness – something I don't suffer from. If I didn't feel so sorry for the poor fellows who, driven by their holy zeal, fell into the trap so helplessly, I'd be reconciled to the whole business. After all, the summer is best enjoyed out here, and if I'd stayed in Petersburg I wouldn't have been able to extricate myself so easily from the affair with Lisabeth, which I'd instigated rather imprudently. Even though Papa and Mama are a touch reactionary, they do have intellect and taste, and are far better company than the brutal characters you love surrounding your antediluvian thick skin with. To ensure peace at the table here, one mustn't challenge Papa too seriously, but on occasion Mama quite enjoys hearing a rebellious opinion and she will defy Papa with a certain panache. He likes this in her, so long as it's kept within respectable limits. But if he emphatically clears his throat or frowns, she will immediately back down, her subordination leading by example. Katya is here too, so it's not merely tolerable, it's positively agreeable.

Our guardian angel has arrived. Mama is convinced that he has the skill to divert all poisons, weapons, sticks of dynamite and other mishaps away from father and onto himself. She has an awfully high opinion of this talented young man. We were expecting someone with a bushy beard, trusty fists and a pompous manner of speaking. Instead he's slim, clean-shaven, reserved; more of an English type. He told me his father was insisting he apply for a professorship – he studied philosophy, you see – but he says he doesn't want to start out on a career and he has a particular dislike of professional philosophers. To force him, his father has stopped all his funds, which is why he accepted this post with us, for which he does not consider himself especially competent. He said, 'I think to begin with I can make myself useful by calming your mother's nerves, a task I do not regard as particularly difficult. She possesses the wonderful quality of being free of scepticism, and will happily regard me as a natural lightning conductor if I make a small effort to present myself as one.' I said, 'Just so long as you don't get bored.' He laughed and said, 'I never get bored. Wherever he is, man is at the centre of a mystery. But, quite apart from that, I love country life and good company, so I'm well provided for here.' He has a penetrating look, and I am convinced that he has already dissected and categorized each one of us with a fair degree of accuracy. He seems inscrutable himself, but despite his apparent coolness I think he's audacious, ambitious and full of passion. It would be a shame if he were to become a professor. I feel he wants more and is capable of more than other people. I suspect his views are no less revolutionary than our own, but so far he has given nothing away about himself in discussion. In fact, it is his objectivity that impresses me the most, especially as it doesn't prevent his conversation from being stimulating. Jessika and Katya, of course, are terribly susceptible to this, although there's no need for you to start getting jealous, you old dinosaur.

Yours, Velya

JESSIKA TO TATYANA

Kremskoye, 7th May

Dear Aunt,

As it's a closely guarded secret that Mama has engaged a secretary for Papa, whose real task is to protect Papa from the bombs he's been threatened with,

I can assume that it's common knowledge. Perhaps it's better for the matter to be widely known, for then the anarchists won't start their bombing, which will make our guardian angel's work easier. You can see that I look with favour upon him; he's already earned my approval as his being here has such a positive influence on Mama's mood. At lunch on the first day Mama asked him what he had dreamed, since she believes the first dream one has in a new house is significant. I think he didn't dream anything at all, but without a moment's hesitation he launched into a long story about how he found himself in a magnificent palace, wandering from one room to another, and described them all in great detail. Finally he came to a chamber which was pitch black inside; as he stood on the threshold he was overcome by an inexplicable trepidation. He hesitated to go on, then composed himself, then paused again before waking up with his heart pounding. Mama's eyes were growing ever bigger. 'It's a good thing you didn't go in,' she said. 'I'm certain there would have been something terrible inside.' 'A bath, perhaps,' Velya said softly, and all of us burst out laughing. As Katya only started when the rest of us had finished, this went on for quite a while. I said, 'Please continue with this dream tonight and take a bath to reassure Mama, for bathing can only be a good omen.' No, Mama said, water was ambiguous; only fire was a definite sign of good luck and she'd dreamed of this last night. Then she recounted her dream; it was so sweet. As she and Papa were getting ready for the night she noticed their beds were ablaze, beautiful flames without any smoke (this is very important!) and she kept blowing, thinking she could extinguish the fire. Papa said, 'Lusinya, stop blowing!' barely able to speak for laughter, and she also started laughing, then woke up laughing. Mama related this dream to Lyu, whose arrival has brought us luck, she said; she calls Lyu our guardian angel. He proceeded to explain where the popular belief in the significance of dreams comes from, why all peoples interpret fire and water in the same way, and what of all this is actually true. I'm afraid I can't describe it to you as elegantly as he did. Papa listened with great interest too, even though he understands nothing of dreams and suchlike, eventually saying with a sigh, 'You'd make the perfect secretary for my wife!' Now I'm going to tell you something delightful that happened at lunch today. I asked Velya whether he wanted some more pudding and he said, as is his wont, 'Thy will be done, Father!' Lyu gave him a look of curiosity, upon which Mama explained that this was Velya's favourite expression, which he always used to mean 'I don't care'. She added, however, that she hoped he would now ditch this nasty habit, because she couldn't suffer any blasphemy. 'Blasphemy?' Velya said in surprise. 'What do you mean by that?' 'Velya,' Mama said in disgust, 'stop pretending you don't know that these words are in the Bible!' 'But, honest to God, I had no idea,' Velya countered. 'If I'd known that the Bible contained such rotten expressions, I'd have given it a read!' Oh, the innocence of it all; the most honest look of surprise beamed from his wide-open eyes. Lyu couldn't stop laughing; I think he's charmed by Velya.

Papa's nerves are holding up well. He grumbled at Ivan once when he thought he was drunk – coincidentally, he wasn't on that occasion – and another time when he thought the rice was burnt, but he hasn't caused a real fuss yet, even though we've been here for four days.

Dearest Auntie, every day I place bunches of thyme, lavender and rosemary in our guest room, not just on the table, but in the chests of drawers and wardrobes, gradually filling it with a lovely homely smell. Please reward my attentiveness by coming to see us.

Affectionately, Jessika

KATYA TO PETER

Kremskoye, 9th May

Dear Peter,

You're a silly billy if you actually took offence at my not having been at home when you wanted to bid me adieu. How could I know that you were coming?

And in any case I was paying a visit to the old general's wife, which is truly no pleasure. Taking offence is so terribly petit bourgeois; I do hope Velya was lying to me. If I didn't find it so outrageous that Papa closed the university, I'd feel happy to be here. I do nothing but eat, sleep, read and cycle. The new secretary is very elegant, even though he has no money, and he's a brilliant man, phenomenally clever. He comes cycling with us too, although he doesn't enjoy it. He finds it old-fashioned and says we ought to travel by motorcar. I think he's absolutely right and we're going to try to persuade Papa to get us one; for the time being we are subscribing to a motoring journal.

Regards, Katya

LYU TO KONSTANTIN

Kremskoye, 10th May

My stay here is fascinating from a psychological view-point. The family has all the virtues and defects of its class. Perhaps one cannot even talk of defects; they merely have the one: belonging to an era that must pass and standing in the way of one that is emerging. When a beautiful old tree has to be felled to make way for a railway line, it's painful to watch; you stand beside it like an old friend, gazing admiringly and in grief until it comes down. It is undeniably a shame about the governor, who is a splendid example of his kind, but I believe that he has already passed his peak. If only he could realize this and resign from his position, or if he did it to avoid imperilling his life, nobody would welcome this more heartily than I. But he is too proud; he believes that only those who work and achieve something have a right to live. He cannot conceive of a life without work, which is why he wants to work and why he believes that if he does what the doctors advise, he will gradually recover his former strength. Recently he fell asleep while sitting at his desk, allowing me to observe him undisturbed. Without those handsome, dark and passionate eyes of his animating it, his face seemed terribly limp and exhausted, although this could not erase the impression of mature virility he gives overall. When he awoke he immediately sat up straight, cast a rapid glance at me and was visibly heartened by the fact that I appeared to have noticed nothing. It is typical of him that he is loath to admit to being tired or sleepy. So he finds it most agreeable that I can relieve him of the small amount of work he is doing during the holiday, or at least mitigate the burden. He tells me this, but he would not like anyone to think that he's too weary to undertake the work on his own; indeed, merely to think it would make him unhappy.

As often with people who in office are regarded as strict and merciless, he is affable in company, infinitely good-natured even, when he encounters affectionate compliance and submission. Insubordination leaves him speechless, as the only thing he feels intuitively is his own will, and he is naive enough to assume that it must be just as authoritative for others. To me he seems like a beautiful and loyal, if a little careless, sun, assiduously sustaining its world. He rises, shines and warms with all his might, harbouring no doubt that the planets fulfil their mission by orbiting him throughout their life. Essentially he doesn't believe in the existence of comets and anomalies, unless they are from within him; I could imagine that the actual desertion of a satellite would send him mad rather than make him angry. In general, his children do as they please, although in theory they refrain from infringing upon his authority, for they are his own children and he is a man of strong instincts, and ultimately he likes his comforts, which is compatible with his industriousness; at home he wants to be at ease.

Velya is a charming young man, although he is out of place here. He has the soul of a Neapolitan fishing boy or a princely favourite, wearing attractive clothes, coming out with striking, bold utterances and drawing little distinction between dreams and real life. The two daughters are not so like twins as I'd first imagined, not even in appearance. Both are on the shorter side, and have masses of blonde hair above their dainty faces. They are as different as a tea rose is from a moss rose.

When Jessika moves, it is as if a soft wind is blowing a fallen leaf through the room; Katya stands firmly on the ground, and anything that fails to get out of her way may well be emphatically cast aside. Jessika is delicate, she is often in pain, and her vulnerability lends her a particular, refined allure; one gets the impression that it would be impossible to embrace the poor creature without hurting her. Katya is healthy, sincere and not at all agitating: a clever, spirited and delightful girl. On occasion Jessika appears to be languishing for something, then she will surprise one with a charming joke, which is never hurtful, but rather like a choice caress. There is something enchanting about developing an influence over these young people, which I'm enjoying for the time being. I have not, however, abandoned my gravity and toughness.

Lyu

Jessika to Tatyana

Kremskoye, 10th May

Dearest Auntie,

You're perturbed by our protector, who is here specifically to give us reassurance? I am entranced by him and my letter reveals a suspicious gaiety? Goodness gracious, of course I find him agreeable; his presence has allayed Mama's fears! Don't worry, dearest Auntie, if he should fall in love it will be with Katya, and I'm sure you don't consider Katya's heart to be as fragile as my own. Or are you concerned that Peter might become jealous? Do you know what? I believe that Katya doesn't really fall in love seriously; she sits with Velya amongst the redcurrant bushes and the two of them eat with the same rapidity they did ten years ago, as if they were going to be awarded a medal for their feat.

Truly, Mama is calmer and happier than she has been for a long time. Good God, when I think back to how she was those last few days in town, the performance she would make if Papa stayed out half an hour longer than she expected! Recently she couldn't find him in his room, nor anywhere else in the house and not in the garden either. She was already starting to get jittery when Mariushka told us that the governor had gone for a walk with his secretary. At once her mood settled and she asked me to join her in a duet, claiming that I sang beautifully, and belting out the tune herself like a nightingale in a romantic novel. This afternoon Papa was still a little drowsy when he was called for tea. Mama picked up her lorgnette, looked at him closely and asked tenderly, 'Why are you so pale, Yegor?' Papa said, 'Finally! I thought you didn't love me any more because it's taken you eight days to ask.' He was teasing her, of course, but if Mama's anxiety, which he always jokes about, were to vanish, he would actually feel neglected. This is what the governor is like.

It's just occurred to me, dearest Auntie, that I have no idea whether your cold has gone for good, nor whether the mysterious, awkward pain in your little finger has subsided, nor whether and when you are coming. The lilac is blooming, the chestnuts are blooming, everything that can bloom is in flower!

Affectionately, Jessika

VELYA TO PETER

Kremskoye, 12th May

Dear Peter,

If you let your jealousy show, you'll make yourself look ridiculous in front of Katya. And what for? To begin with you might still be jealous of me, but you're not refined enough for that. Lyu is courting Jessika – that's to say he gazes at her and commands her with his eyes, for of course she falls immediately for this. Lyu is an extraordinary man, soulless, you could even say, if it's possible to use that word to describe an element that is pure force. I expect he would have no qualms about making Jessika unhappy, or any other girl for that matter. If you have the courage to abandon yourself to him completely, you also need the courage to allow yourself to be destroyed. And why do the girls dive so eagerly into the light? Whatever the reason, it is their own decision, like with the moths that burn their wings. Moreover, Lyu would never sacrifice a girl to his vanity, as most of us do. He only destroys them incidentally, as the sun does. They mustn't get too close to him, but of course they cannot stop themselves. Katya is, thank God, different, which I love about her, although I shouldn't want all girls to be like her.

Yesterday Katya and I discovered a Turkish confectioner in the village, who had the most wonderful wares: red and sticky and translucent and rubbery. He seems to be a real Turk, for I've never eaten anything so sweet before. I imagine the further south-east you go, the more wonderful the sweets become. Katya and I kept eating; the Turk was expressionless as he watched us with his large cow-like eyes. Eventually we couldn't eat any more and I said, 'We've got to stop now.' 'Don't you have any more money?' he asked; I fancy he regarded us as children. I said, 'I feel sick.' His yellow face remained unmoved. Had we exploded before his very eyes I doubt he would have so much as twitched.

We met a very lovely girl in the village with whom we used to play when we were children. Back then we found her awfully ugly because of her red hair, which we would tease her about; now I found her devilishly nice. I called out to her, 'Anetta, you're not ugly any more!' She immediately retorted, 'Velya, you're not blind any more!' I couldn't take it any further as Katya was there, but I gave her a nod and she understood me.

Velya

Lusinya to Tatyana

Kremskoye, 13th May

Dear Tatyana,

Please tell me why you're convinced my daughters must be falling in love with Lyu? Till now I've regarded them as far too immature for love; Katya, after all, is really still a child. But since you've now drawn my attention to the matter, I can see that Lyu is dangerous: masculine, courageous, clever, interesting, eye-catching – everything that might impress a young girl. At this point, however, I must praise him for behaving in rather a reserved fashion towards my two little ones. Maybe he's already engaged. I've certainly noticed Jessika's admiration for him; whenever he speaks, her eyes fix on him, she is more talkative than normal and brimming with the loveliest ideas. I didn't think there was anything bad in this; on the contrary, I've been delighted to see her so happy. Tatyana, if you wish to invite her and she wants to come, then I shan't stand in the way. It may even be better if she does. My poor little Jessika; the idea that she's in love with him! If he didn't love her she would suffer, and perhaps even more if he did. No, he is not the man for her. He understands everything, but always remains sober-minded, never dropping his guard. He has no appreciation of trivial things or frivolity, or if he does, then it's like collecting plants in a herbarium. He cannot give of himself, he only consumes. I believe him to be highly capable in many fields, and am sure he'll be a terribly famous man one day. But whatever his future, my little girl would struggle to breathe in the thin, lofty air he needs.

What I find strange about this man is that he evidently has an active interest in all of us, he appears receptive to our qualities, he accepts the trust we place in him as a matter of course, and yet gives nothing of himself. It's not that he isn't open; every question you might put to him he answers candidly and thoroughly. It might even be misleading to call him withdrawn, for he talks rather a lot and always about things that are really important to him. And yet you never feel as if you know what he's like inside. It's already crossed my mind that there might be secrets in his life which compel him to be reserved, but it doesn't bother me, as I'm sure that there's nothing bad. Recently we were talking about lies. Lyu said that in certain circumstances lies were a weapon in life's struggle, no worse than any other; only lying to oneself was contemptible. Velya said, 'Lying to oneself? But I'd never believe me.' Lyu gave a laugh of joy and I, too, couldn't help laughing, but I felt duty-bound to tell Velya that it was a bad joke. 'But we can't crack better ones here,' my boy said, 'otherwise Katya won't understand them.' Well, what I really wanted to tell you was that I am truly convinced that Lyu would never lie to himself, and for me that's the fundamental thing. The principle may be dangerous, but it's reasonable for a person of importance.

Dear sister of my beloved husband, if I didn't have the children around me, I could now imagine we were on our honeymoon. If only we never had to return to the city! Yegor has resumed playing the piano, for he cannot go a moment without being occupied, while I, who certainly can, listen to him and fall into a reverie. Do you recall the time when I called him my immortal? Sometimes, when I look at him now, I'm struck by the feeling that he's become something else. It's not the white hair, which has now overtaken the black, nor the deep shadows that often sit beneath his eyes, nor the harsh lines that darken his face. No, it's something nameless that surrounds his entire being. Once I had to leap up all of a sudden and hurry away, because tears were pouring from my eyes, and in the bedroom I cried into the pillow, 'My immortal! Oh, my immortal!' I don't consider it strange that there are mad people around, but it's lamentable that even the most rational individuals can have fits of madness.

Yours, Lusinya

LYU TO KONSTANTIN

Kremskoye, 15th May

Dear Konstantin,

I might have predicted you'd react like this, but I hope you will have no cause to in the future. You make it sound as if I've come here to undertake a psychological study. You think I'm developing a keen sense of family life. You say I might just as well be visiting my aunt in Odessa and much more besides. What do you want? Did you expect me to pounce on my victim like a hungry cannibal, a hate-filled love rival or a cheated husband? We were agreed that we would not proceed like those fanatical ruffians who, when executing an assassination, seem to be more bent on disposing of their own lives than those of their targets. We wanted to achieve our goal without risking our lives, our freedom, maybe even our reputations, for we have more to achieve and we know that we are difficult to replace. If time were pressing, I would have acted differently, but the students' trial only starts at the beginning of August, until which time the governor will be on holiday here. I therefore have three months, of which barely a fortnight has passed. I am taking a good look around, acquainting myself with the people, my surroundings, and waiting for an opportunity. Of course, I could have already killed the governor, had I so wished; I often find myself alone with him, in the house, as well as in the garden and the woods. But in that case I would have acted wrongly. At this moment in time when I am much valued, almost held in affection, and yet remain a stranger, suspicion could be raised against me. But in a few weeks I shall be as a member of the family, and suspicion will be out of the question. I believe I wrote recently that I sat beside him for a few minutes while he was sleeping. I gazed at the side of his face that was turned towards me – the broad, black eyebrows, a sign of great virility; the prominent aquiline nose; fire and nobility in every single one of his lines. Another key feature of his personality seems to be a passion tempered by genteel sensibility. What a wonderful man! As I watched him I thought how I should much rather make this head receptive to my thoughts, my opinions, than destroy it with a bullet. You must consider that I could avoid killing this man if I were to succeed in controlling, influencing him. But I will state right here and now that I regard this a very remote possibility. In small matters he's like wax, in important ones like iron. If he is resolved on something, neither fear nor love can change his mind; at least, that's how I see it at present.

The boy is different: he is so indolent that he is grateful if one stands up for him; one just needs to do it with discrimination. He is astonishingly open-minded. In no way does he appear to be a prisoner of tradition; something about him suggests there is nothing tying him to the past, his family or his motherland. I cannot help recalling an old fairy tale in which a parentless boy appears as the sun's child. His golden-brown skin brings to mind this story too. In conversation with him I virtually speak my mind; he is so unprejudiced that it doesn't even occur to him to wonder how I could have taken a post with his father given the views I hold. He appears to find it only natural that a man of reason can think as I do, while also playing any role that suits his taste and is useful to get him ahead. I like the boy and I'm most glad not to have to harm him. Katya thinks like her brother, maybe in part out of love for him. For a girl, she is highly intelligent and insightful, but no matter how sensibly she talks, she is still like a sweet little bird chirruping on a perch. I find this enchanting about her.

Konstantin, do not reproach me again. If there were accusations to be made I should level them myself, and for this reason no one else has the right to do so.

Lyu

JESSIKA TO TATYANA

Kremskoye, 15th May

Oh, most gracious Auntie, you have invited me to visit you! I kiss your hand in gratitude. And I may even come when you're not expecting it. But, dearest Auntie, do you not know that I have duties here? I cannot leave just like that. There is a household to be run and, as you know, even the best servants need to be inspired by a higher being. I pity that poor cook who, with our fivefold whimsies, would have no backup if I were to leave. Papa adores stuffed tomatoes, but not tomato sauce, which Mama is very fond of; and whereas Velya has a passion for tomatoes in salad, Katya only eats them raw. Katya won't eat sweet rice, Papa won't touch spicy rice and I don't like rice pudding. None of us eats cabbage, but we want green vegetables every day. I could go on like this for pages. No cook could possibly keep all that in her head, and ours cannot read. If I went away, Mama would have to think of everything – for it would never occur to Katya – and I'd be very sorry. She spends her days wandering around the house, and is pleased to have her husband to herself, as well as in safety. Now is not the time to burden her with silly everyday concerns.

You'll think I'm just an insignificant little girl! But they'd soon notice if they weren't served their cup of tea or coffee with precisely the amount of sugar and milk or lemon that each of them likes, or if the orange slices did not fly onto the dish thinly cut and without pips, as they are used to, or if the pencils, scissors and parasols that they lose or misplace were not found by me at just the right moment! This is what I do! Why don't you come and see for yourself just how indispensable I am?

If you now think that I ought to be rewarded and compensated, Aunt Tatyana, then send me some purple batiste for a blouse and matching trim and lace. I've nothing here light enough to wear in this heat. You have the finest taste of anybody, my lovely Auntie, so please acquire these things for me.

Your grateful Jessika

VELYA TO PETER

Kremskoye, 17th May

Dear Peter,

I was wrong: *au fond* Lyu is a revolutionary; it's just that there's something which makes his opinions tower above average ones. How can I make you comprehend this, my dear megatherium? He thinks, while at the same time standing above his thoughts. He doesn't regard the things he thinks and wishes for as the ultimate, the absolute. This is why he also stands aside from party politics; he gazes out over the parties. He says that the new generation is right vis-à-vis the older one, although viewed in isolation it is almost less in the right than the older generation. You won't understand this of course because you lack self-irony, both the concept of it and the trait itself. Your lot have no idea how amusing it is when you get worked up about how degenerate the old culture has become and yet have not the faintest idea of what culture actually means. Don't get worked up, don't start roaring, you old dinosaur, I'm absolutely on your side. My father is priceless. He regards Lyu as a terribly nice, intelligent and entertaining man; his sharp eye goes no further. He cannot conceive of the idea that a man in honest clothing, who behaves politely and refrains from contradicting him, could possibly move outside of his system. Mama is much less, how should I put it, wrapped up in herself. She, at least, can clearly see that she's a long way from understanding every facet of Lyu's character; she senses something unfamiliar, even though she cannot apprehend it. Recently she told him that the position he occupies in our house was not commensurate with his talents, knowledge and efficiency. Nor was the remuneration, she added; he should never have accepted it. Lyu said he'd hoped that being a private secretary would afford him the free time he needs to complete a philosophical work, which is his next aim. Mama turned a deep shade of red and said surely he must be disappointed, as we were forever making demands of him. I think Lyu had completely forgotten that he's here to intercept bombs and murderers, while Mama thinks he's wearing himself out with this difficult to define activity. Since then she's often invited him to retire to his room and work, and she has a tendency to think Papa's being very demanding when he wishes to dictate the occasional letter to him in his spare time. He could easily get himself a typewriter, she said. You could hardly say that Mama exploits people.

We are currently urging father to buy a motorcar, and he's very close to doing so. At the dinner table we're always discussing the last automobile race and debating whether it's cheaper with petrol or electricity. Lyu wondered whether we might not wait until we could acquire a navigable aircraft. Papa was most taken with the idea, and once he'd calculated the costs of such a purchase, a motorcar seemed terribly ordinary and petit bourgeois by comparison. Lyu is not a bit musical. He claims music is a primitive art form, at least the music we know up till now. One day it could possibly be different; Richard Wagner has given vague intimations of this. But he says the musical offerings in our family are primitive. I think he's absolutely right, especially as far as Papa is concerned. His playing is beautiful, but in the same way that the forest rustles or the wind whooshes: there's something demonic about it. Obsession is not a sign of culture, however. On the other hand, Lyu seems to have a lot of time for the primitive. He thinks that Jessika's voice sounds like the red of dawn emerging in the pallid first light of the east. I think Jessika has a good voice too, to me it sounds like a harp, but I've never really had much time for singing in itself; after all, music really begins with the symphony. Do not imagine for a moment that you're a superior being because you're unmusical. With you it's a vacuum.

Velya

KATYA TO TATYANA

Kremskoye, 17th May

Dear Auntie,

Jessika forgot to ask you to buy for us the score of *Tristan und Isolde*, or have someone else do it. Papa is against the idea; he says musical scores can be borrowed too! Does that sort of thing exist? Oh, please don't bother finding out; borrowing books from a lending library is rather vulgar, and scores are books, aren't they? Deep down Papa is just annoyed that we're interested in Wagner; he's so biased. He doesn't even want to get to know Wagner; he's determined to find him dreadful from the outset. Well, if Wagner had lived a few hundred years ago and composed church music like Palestrina – oh, I know it sounds stupid, but I've written it now, and you understand what I'm saying. Of course Beethoven's songs to his distant lover, which Papa always sings, are beautiful, but they're not an expression of our time and our lives. Anyway, Auntie Tatyana, you'll send us *Tristan*

und Isolde, won't you? Please do so quickly. Peter can
go and get it.

Yours, Katya

Lʏᴜ ᴛᴏ Kᴏɴsᴛᴀɴᴛɪɴ

Kremskoye, 20th May

Dear Konstantin,

Your letter induced me to commit an indiscretion,
but it would be a poor general who was unable to cor-
rect, or even exploit, a false move. The rumour that
the students' trial is going to be held immediately, and
thus the governor is returning to Petersburg at once,
must be unfounded, for he would be the first to know
and consequently I would be in the picture too. All
the same, I entertained the possibility yesterday and
have prepared myself in case I need to act rapidly
and suddenly. I told myself that it would not be easy
to find an opportunity during the daytime, especially
not one that would be favourable to me. At night-
time I could sedate him and his wife – they sleep in
the same room – kill him with a stab to the heart
and then retire to my bed unnoticed. There would
be no finger of suspicion pointing at me in particular. During the day, however, no one could intrude
on the governor without somebody – that's to say

me – noticing. Myriad unpredictable disruptions might occur in the daytime; at night, the circumstances are certain, clear. Essentially, the viability of my plan is dependent on how lightly the governor and his wife sleep, so I resolved to find out as soon as I could. I put on a coat and tiptoed to their bedroom, which is separated from mine by a dressing room with a connecting bathroom and cloakroom. Barely had I set foot over the threshold than I saw Mrs von Rasimkara hurrying towards me. I'll admit that at that moment I almost lost my head; seeing before me this woman looking so strange, so beautiful, so different from during the day – it took my breath away. In her face was an expression of both horror and unhesitating determination, which, as soon as she recognized me, gave way to relief, surprise and, I should say, a feeling for the comic nature of the situation. Indeed, for an instant I could think and feel nothing save for how ravishing she was. She swiftly dragged me back into the dressing room and said in a whisper that I'd given her such a fright, she'd thought I was a murderer. What had happened? Was anything wrong? Was I sleepwalking? I told her she needn't worry in the slightest; nothing had happened. I'd awoken, thought I'd heard a noise and just wanted to make sure that everything was all right with them. This was something I'd often done, I said, because I regarded it as part of my duty, but she'd never noticed before. I added that it might be better not to mention the incident to her husband. Of course not, she said, she was pleased he hadn't woken up. Then she squeezed my hand, gave me a nod and a smile, and went back to her bedroom.

This was a treacherous moment, and I was unable to get to sleep again until morning. When she stood before me, smiling, I found her ravishing, while also thinking that I would have to kill her. This thought occurred to me so vividly that I felt as if I were screaming from my eyes, 'I am your killer because I am his killer. You will always be at his side, your body will throw itself in front of his when the time comes, which is why you must die with him.' The peculiar look she gave me seemed to say, 'I understand you. It is my destiny; I accept it.'

In one respect I gained something from my unfortunate endeavour. Now I know that the governor sleeps deeply. I have impressed upon her the idea that I occasionally enter their bedroom for the protection of her husband. If she were to see me come in, bend over her, she would not harbour any suspicion until the very last moment; rather she would gaze at me expectantly with wide eyes. On the other hand, I have learned that I have an aversion to this kind of deed. I should resort to it only in the most extreme of circumstances. Another way will be found that is more promising for me. In any case you have no need to worry. I may have acted rashly, but I nipped in the bud any bad consequences.

Lyu

VELYA TO PETER

Kremskoye, 20th May

Dear Peter,

Today I feel as if I'm in a madhouse. Last night Mama heard something which, it later became apparent, was nothing. In spite of the fact that it all turned out to be her imagination, she has a tear-stained face and she jumps at the slightest noise. Papa has fits of rage, which we are supposed to respect as nervousness. Earlier he rang for Mariushka, because she'd left the electric light on in the cloakroom. He made such a row that I could hear it in the garden, and virtually behaved as if this electric light would bring ruin on our whole family. It transpired afterwards that it was he who'd switched it on and forgotten to turn it off again. Now it was Katya's turn to start shouting. She said it was outrageous that the entire household was in floods of tears on Papa's account; how could the servants possibly respect him if he behaved like that? She asked me whether I didn't think the same, to which I replied, 'Thy will be done, Papa.' At this her rage suddenly switched to me, which fortunately had us all soon laughing. Papa said he would have to apologize to Mariushka because he'd done her an injustice, and to this end he headed for the servants' quarters. We wanted to go with him to be present at the scene, but Mama forbade us, regarding it as unseemly. I'd found the whole thing amusing from the outset and cannot understand how Katya gets annoyed.

Katya to Peter

Of course I get annoyed. Velya cannot take anything seriously because he is too idle. Naturally it's outrageous that a man such as Papa, who cannot control himself, closes the university because the students are defending their rights. It's outrageous that a man can enjoy such power; this fact alone spells doom for our circumstances. Please see if you can find some teachers who will give us – and anyone else who wishes to take part – private tuition. We could hold the lessons at your house, nobody can forbid that. I don't think we should put up with this state of affairs. Whether I finish a few years earlier or later does not bother me in the slightest, but it should at least be dependent on me. And if this doesn't work then I'd like to go away, abroad. Having to live in Russia has become insufferable. I get no response from Velya; he's completely gormless and shows no interest in anything I say or suggest. I accept that if you must, you must, but first one should try to see whether there's another way.

Katya

LUSINYA TO TATYANA

24th May

Oh my goodness! So the children have written to say that we're on edge again? If you promise not to breathe a word to anyone else, I'll tell you how it happened. You know I'm an anxious, jumpy soul, and you also know that – unfortunately – I have good reason to be so. I'll admit that I would be like that anyway, but this doesn't alter the fact that the reason exists. Well, a few nights ago I woke up to find a man in the doorway to our bedroom. Naturally I thought he'd come to kill Yegor, so I rushed straight at him in protection – I had no time to think about it. It was only a moment, then I recognized Lyu. Yes, it was Lyu. The abrupt dissipation of fear and dread was so liberating that I almost burst out laughing; I could have embraced him. But afterwards, as I lay in bed, the consequences of having my nerves strained manifested themselves: the tears came to my eyes and I couldn't stop crying. I was overcome by a sense of unease, far more disconcerting than the fear I'd felt earlier; I found it so sinister that Lyu had been sleepwalking. For I cannot find any explanation for what happened other than that he's a somnambulist. He gave me a different account; he said he regarded it as his duty to check from time to time that everything is all right with us, and claimed he'd often been in our bedroom before, especially when he thought he'd heard a noise. It sounds perfectly plausible and perhaps you'll say that I ought to find it reassuring to have him watch over us so devotedly. Previously I would have thought so too, but now I see that the idea of a situation is very different from the situation itself. The fact that all of a sudden there's a man standing in our room at night, whether because he's sleepwalking or for any other reason, isn't alarming to me, but I do find it most sinister. I cannot sleep any more, because I'm always thinking that he'll be standing there at any moment, looking at me with his strange grey eyes which seem to penetrate everything. The moment I've fallen asleep I wake again with a start, terrified. It struck me that he might climb in through the open window; surely you know that sleepwalkers can wander everywhere, even on the edge of the roof. And I find this thought sinister. There's nothing I can do to combat it. I'd really like to close the window, but Yegor doesn't want to. He says it's nonsense and I ought to banish such morbid thoughts. Snakes can crawl up walls, he said, sleepwalkers cannot. What do you think? I once read that the law of gravity didn't apply to sleepwalkers. God only knows!

Unfortunately I related the entire episode to Yegor, who didn't wake up and heard nothing. He's in good spirits, but my fearfulness makes him slightly impatient, because he cannot empathize with it himself. What also irritate him are the circumstances that demand a certain wariness, and wisely so. With his temperament, he cannot bear to see this.

The children know nothing of the incident, for I should not like it to be discussed at the dinner table. It also seems to me to be more considerate of Lyu, to whom we owe so much. If the rumour went around that he is a sleepwalker, it would harm his standing. Nor should it become known that he enters our room at night to check on us.

Katya, my golden child, is an incorrigible little devil. At every opportunity she complains about the closure of the university, even though she knows that she ought not to touch on political and business matters at the moment, because it vexes Yegor. I wonder whether your Peter will ever be able to cope with her? It says a lot about him that he imagines he will. He has inherited nothing from you, dearest; he is just like your husband, who after all succeeded in making an impression on you, didn't he? My little one is still too much of a child to be impressed by anything in this world. I should wish that he might succeed in winning her heart, if only so that she could have you as a mother-in-law. And his solidity and groundedness would be perfect for her too. Jessika is blossoming, the countryside is doing her the world of good; she is our Hebe with the rosy cheeks. I do hope the little night-time interlude will not disturb me for much longer.

Love and kisses, Lusinya

Jessika to Tatyana

Kremskoye, 25th May

Dearest Auntie,

It's a good thing I stayed here. Mama is currently in a phase where all her attention is focused on her Yegor, our father. And there must be a spirit hovering above the house. Just imagine, Auntie, our motorcar is arriving in a few days' time. At the last moment Mama asserted that it's dangerous and we'd be better off without one. This was the final little nudge Papa needed to make up his mind. For he said that we should ignore Mama's anxiety; if she didn't grow up now she'd soon be too old for it. Papa doesn't want a chauffeur, as that would make the whole affair too expensive, and besides, he doesn't care for strangers in the house. Ivan will have to learn how to drive. Velya said, 'The gaffer steers our carriage into the ditch. Where's he going to end up with the motorcar?' Papa told Velya not to exaggerate, Ivan was not always drunk, he was frequently sober too. With a sigh, Mama expressed her hope that he'd be sober for our outings in the motorcar. I suggested we make excursions only occasionally, so they'd be certain to coincide with Ivan's frequent periods of sobriety. It made perfect sense to Mama, but Katya got hot under the collar, saying that this wasn't why we were getting a motorcar, she wanted to go for a drive every day, and so on. Fortunately Lyu intervened, mentioning that he'd dabbled a little in driving and was keen to learn more, so he could replace Ivan from time to time. Afterwards, when Papa wasn't there, Velya said, 'All the same, Papa would rather drive with Ivan because he believes that God looks after drunkards.' That's a saying, you know.

There's something else I have to tell you about Ivan. Yesterday lunchtime Velya said he'd asked him what he thought of Lyu, because he'd noticed that Ivan couldn't abide him. Apparently Ivan was evasive, unwilling to say anything. Velya said surely he found Lyu friendly, even-handed, helpful, bright, able – all of which Ivan conceded. Finally, however, he said, 'He's too educated for my liking.' Velya replied that Papa was educated as well, upon which Ivan narrowed his eyes, shook his head and said, 'Yes he is, on the surface, but deep down he's a good man like the rest of us.' All of us laughed, especially Lyu, who was delighted by the comment, seeing in it great profundity. Lyu doesn't ask whether someone likes him or not; that's what I admire about him.

Dear Auntie, I'm singing Tristan, Isolde, Brangäne, King Marke and a few other heroic figures. Can you picture me in full flow? Papa just cast a reluctant glance at the score, and of course I only sing when he's out of earshot.

Yours, Jessika

LYU TO KONSTANTIN

Kremskoye, 27th May

Dear Konstantin,

You think that I might fulfil my mission with the help of the motorcar? Indeed, if it could be so arranged that the governor broke his neck and I my wrist! Do you know how that might be achieved? The thought had occurred to me, of course, the moment the motorcar was first discussed, and I spoke in favour of acquiring one. I also proffered my services as a chauffeur, which was warmly applauded. Besides the aforementioned difficulty, however, another disadvantage of this strategy is that I should lose a lot of time practising my driving, without any enjoyment on my part. I am no sportsman; I do not permit myself to expend much time and effort on such things. I would be interested in piloting an aircraft, but that is work, not sport, and has all manner of scholarly uses, both principal and secondary. I shall, nonetheless, familiarize myself with the motorcar, as I might conceivably need it for a rapid escape.

I have had another idea which I feel has great promise. If possible I should like not to be personally involved in the act of killing, which means a machine would have to play my role. It now occurs to me that this could be a typewriter. I shall furnish you with more detail when my plan has come to greater fruition. I may well need your wise help to ensure that the machine is adapted for purpose without the manufacturer finding out.

Mrs von Rasimkara is a changed woman since that night: pale, almost shy, and permanently at her husband's side. It may be the case that my actions have doubled her apprehensiveness, because she was forced to conclude that I believed her husband to be in great danger. Perhaps she has not been sleeping well since. Before then, my confidence and insouciance had a calming effect on her. A certain reserve – which she is not so much deliberately showing me as letting slip against her will – could be down to the fact that the memory of our night-time encounter, which was so peculiar, so fleeting, yet so arresting, and which only the two of us know about, makes her feel embarrassed or at least moves her in a particular way. She harbours no suspicion of me, of that I am quite sure. On the contrary, she treats me with a greater degree of friendliness and deference. As she is almost always in the company of her husband, I am obliged to spend more time with the children, whose close friend and confidant I have become.

You must not leave Petersburg for the time being, as I may need your help with the typewriter.

Lyu

VELYA TO PETER

Kremskoye, 28th May

Dear Peter,

Today we almost had a family catastrophe, in which of course I played no active part. At the table Katya started talking about what's happening at the university. She pointed out that to her it makes no difference as she has no need to earn a livelihood, but for most students it's disastrous to be forced to interrupt their studies indefinitely. Still relatively calm and composed, Papa said it was certainly unlucky for many, which was why those who had brought this misfortune on their fellow students with their inflammatory behaviour ought to be judged even more harshly. This really set Katya off! Like an artificial waterfall switched into action! How typical of unjust despots, she said, to malign the victims and offload their own guilt onto them! Demodov and the others were martyrs, she added. They might be executed or sent to Siberia, but they could never be stripped of their glory for having acted with courage and selfless-ness. Moreover, almost everybody shared her opinion, she added. You, for example, planned to make a stand against the Cossacks too; it was only by chance that you were held up on your way to the university, otherwise Papa could have sent you to the mines as well, she said. Eventually Mama managed to interrupt her by saying that Papa definitely would have if he had considered it his duty, for surely Katya didn't doubt that Papa was guided by his sense of duty, which is why she mustn't criticize his actions. I said, 'If he had your bird brain, of course he would act differently,' upon which she gave me a withering look. Papa was quite pale and his eyebrows looked like a jagged black thunderbolt: incredibly atmospheric. If this hadn't been about Katya, a raging storm would have erupted, sweeping away the entire table and all the chairs; as it was he managed to control himself to some extent. Moreover, Lyu's presence averts any catastrophe; his masterful calmness somehow dissipates all accumulated electricity – either that, or he has so much strength that he can absorb it all himself and render it harmless. He sat there as coolly as Talleyrand, proving that all of us were right, with the result that everyone fell silent, feeling satisfied. He said that obviously there was injustice in the order to close the university, but that was why it could be entirely fair within the system to which it belonged. He was not endorsing this system; he said it had become obsolete, but while it still existed one must work within its rules. Papa looked at Lyu with interest and slight surprise, asking him what he meant when he said that he didn't endorse the system. No government was perfect, Papa continued, because human nature was flawed. But in his opinion it was better to ensure that everyone did his duty rather than uncover the defects in the system. Lyu said that without the principle that everyone must do his duty, no social system could survive.

He believed that the fault of the existing system was that it failed to cultivate a sense of duty, because it had imposed rules and regulations in its place. Such a strategy was justified for a primitive culture, but these days the people were no longer a herd; they were individuals. No connoisseur of art could fail to admire Byzantine painting, with its rigid forms; we might even believe, nay desire, that one day we would return to it via some circuitous route. But surely nobody would wish to reverse the level of social development back to that stage.

He spoke so graciously, gallantly and almost affectionately that Papa became quite animated, vigorously agreeing with everything. I fancy he believed himself to be entirely of the same mind as Lyu.

Thus things had sorted themselves out again at the table, but then Katya's bottled-up anger towards Lyu poured out. He'd behaved abominably, she said; he ought to have supported her because he thought exactly as she did. What he said may have been frightfully elegant, but she didn't understand it, nor did she *wish* to understand it; it can only have been rhetoric to hide his true opinions. She fully expected me to be duplicitous and cowardly, but she'd imagined him to be a prouder man. She was quite adorable, like a fretful little bird, ruffling up its crest, pecking with its beak and cheeping in the highest possible tones. Lyu evidently found her adorable too, for he reacted very benignly to her nonsense. I left in the middle of this because my village beauty was waiting for me.

I brought Papa back a selection of the finest sweet-meats the Turk has to offer. He found them excellent and said he'd guessed I must have a particular reason for bicycling to the village so often. Moreover, he ate more of them than I did, without feeling sick at all. He truly is an admirable man; I'm a decadent fellow by contrast. But it's impossible to compare him to Lyu. He's like a handsome dagger with an ornate grip and a scabbard colourfully decorated with precious stones, as you sometimes see on display in museums. Lyu is like Apollo's simple bow, which never shoots a stray arrow. Unadorned, slim, flexible, handsome on account of its complete functionality, a picture of divine power, accuracy and unscrupulousness. For goodness' sake, I'm writing to a Silurian sloth, not a Greek sophisticate. Do not torture yourself with the pervasiveness of my poetic images and don't crow if they're lame. A lame Achilles still arrives before a brontosaurus that's stuck in the sand.

Velya

KATYA TO PETER

Kremskoye, 30th May

Dear Peter,

We are not engaged and I've told you before that I'll never marry you, but I know that you still think about it, which is why I wish to tell you something. I have now met the man I will marry, should I ever come to marry. The only one I could love. Do not ask who he is; don't ask any more questions at all. There was no need for me to tell you. I'm only doing so because I like you, because I consider you my friend, and because you have regarded me as your future wife ever since you were a child. Naturally there's nothing I can do about that. Nobody is to know this apart from you.

Katya

LUSINYA TO TATYANA

Kremskoye, 2nd June

My dear Tatyana,

From somewhere or other, a slight shadow is descending upon our summer, which has been nothing but beautiful. Perhaps because it is so beautiful it must bear the sign of its earthly nature. At the moment I am especially concerned about Jessika; I can no longer deny that she's in love with Lyu. Without her being aware of it, her entire being is drawn to him. You might say she's a sort of sundial from which one can always pinpoint the position of her sun. Indeed, there is something sun-like about him; it is as if he radiates a life-generating force, which can cause life to wither too, of course.

He has a wholesome influence on Velya and Katya; he inspires them to think, to attain a higher level of intellectual activity. But I fear his rays are too hot for my little Jessika. She needs warmth, but mustn't stand in the middle of the fire. Or at least that's how it appears to me. Sometimes I feel that not only is she attracted to him, but he harbours a slight affection for her too. Does he love her? Whenever I believe this to be the case I cannot help but feel joy inside, for a mother senses her child's every pain and pleasure. But would this be a desirable state of affairs? Would it spell happiness for her? Lyu's opinions and – more importantly – his whole world view differ markedly from Yegor's and my own, I can feel this. As far as his upbringing and lifestyle are concerned, he is also more distant from the children than they themselves believe. Maybe I'm doing him an injustice, but could we really live together as a family in the long term? And what would Yegor say? He has nothing against Lyu – he is free of common prejudices – but he'd like to marry our girls off to men with whose way of living he is familiar, with whom we could become one big family. And then, my dearest, there is his sleepwalking! For me that is almost the most dreadful thing. O God, I know it's so silly, but sometimes I wish Lyu had never come to us, or that he'd leave again.

Afternoon

Lyu really is an uncanny individual! He has eyes that can read one's heart. I had just written that last sentence when he came and told me how happy he was here with us, and sensed, too, that we liked him. He felt superfluous, however, and thought it would be for the best if he left, so he'd come to discuss the matter with me. He spoke with such trust, such simplicity; he sounded almost like a child. I was quite moved and said that although my fear for my husband had indeed gradually subsided, he, Lyu, was also engaged here as a secretary. My husband is unable to write himself at the moment – he's suffering from writer's cramp – and he'd hate to have to get used to another man, nor would he be likely to find another with his, Lyu's, education and knowledge. Lyu said he'd already thought about this and that surely the most sensible solution for my husband would be to acquaint himself with a typewriter, to free him from dependence on anyone; after all, there were many correspondences he'd prefer remained secret. I thought this a capital idea – I really do find him a terribly sensible man – and said that Yegor could certainly acquire a typewriter, but it would probably be quite a while before he got to grips with it, if he had any inclination to do so, and even then the machine would not replace him altogether. Of course, if he wished to leave for another reason, that would be quite a different matter. To which he said that if life were about being happy, all his efforts would be focused on staying with us permanently. He'd found a sort of happiness with us that he'd never previously thought possible; he'd accumulated some indelible impressions. But he regarded man's purpose, or his at least, to be active, to work, to pursue great goals. He was like a horse, he said, that must follow the trumpet call to battle, no matter how comfortable it felt beside its manger full of hay. And he thought he'd heard the call of the trumpet in the distance. 'Do you have anything particular in mind?' I asked. 'Do you wish to leave us immediately?' No, he said, that wasn't what he'd meant. He'd only wanted to hear from me that his presence here was unnecessary, and I'd been candid enough to admit this to him. Now he would ponder where to go. In the meantime, my husband could obtain a typewriter and try to acquire a taste for it.

So you see, Tatyana, now I'm troubled that it's come to this. My little Jessika! Do you know what I think? It's on account of Jessika that he wants to leave. He must have noticed that she loves him. Either the feeling is not mutual or, aware of his poverty and dependence, he does not wish to propose and considers it his duty to avoid her. Such noble behaviour, and the manner in which he deals with the situation is particularly refined. He's made no insinuations, made nothing difficult, kept everything smooth. I've never found him so endearing and I feel Jessika's pain, but now that I can see the conflict – if one exists at all – can be resolved, my heart is less heavy. What a letter! Has your patience lasted till the end?

Your sister-in-law, Lusinya

JESSIKA TO TATYANA

7th June

Dearest Aunt,

You say you haven't had any news from us for a while? Why, I feel as if I wrote to you only yesterday; these summer days are passing by at such a pace! Especially when they're harnessed to a motorcar! Lyu has taken us out for a ride once, but not for long because he still lacks confidence. Our Ivan is even less capable than he, although he drives around for several hours a day. Papa would like to drive too, but Mama doesn't want him to, as she says it would strain his nerves. She claims to know for certain that two-thirds of all chauffeurs go mad or commit suicide due to shredded nerves. Although Papa tried to protest, we clamoured in unison that he had to keep himself well for the sake of the country and his family, and at that he gave in, for the time being at least. He has another pastime now: the typewriter.

Yesterday evening after dinner we sat out on the veranda. It was so beautiful, as only it can be here: above us in the blackness of the sky the damp stars shimmered, and the pale birches around us glowed in the darkness of the earth. We sat in silence, each of us dreaming his own dreams, until Mama asked Lyu – because of course he knows everything – to tell us what sorts of snakes there were in this area. He instantly reeled off a list of Latin names and said they were all adders and vipers: harmless, non-venomous creatures. I wondered whether these names actually existed, but Mama took it all as gospel truth and seemed very relieved. For Papa had recently said that nothing but snakes could climb the smooth walls of a house, and since then she'd been unable to banish from her mind the idea of a firm, smooth, slippery snake's body pulling itself up the outside wall. Often this stopped her sleeping at night. Velya said he couldn't understand people being frightened of snakes; he found them beautiful, graceful, colourful, mysterious, dangerous things, and he would never be able to fall in love with a woman who didn't have something of the snake about them. 'Fool!' Katya said, and Lyu said that I had a few snake-like characteristics, namely mysteriousness and the ability to glide silently. Then he told a southern Russian fairy tale about a really horrible snake. Once upon a time a magician was in love with a king's daughter who was locked up in a tall tower. At midnight, in the form of a snake, he would slither up the tower and through the window into her bedchamber, where he would reassume his human form, wake her and remain in her arms until morning. One night, however, the king's daughter did not go to sleep, but waited up for him. All of a sudden, in the white light of the moon, she saw in the middle of the window the black head of a snake, flat and triangular on an upright neck, gazing at her. She got such a fright that she fell back onto the bed without a sound and died. At that moment there was a loud ringing at the garden gate, where we have an old, rusty bell pull that has sunk into oblivion because practically nobody ever uses it. Papa stood to go to the gate and see what was happening. Mama leapt up too and looked pleadingly at Lyu, implying that he should be the one to confront the murderer if there was one lurking for Papa. And because it's a bit of an effort for Papa to get up and into his stride, and Lyu is a fast runner, our guardian angel got there first and met the delivery man carrying a crate. He said that deliveries were supposed to have stopped for the day, but the postmaster had said the crate was from St Petersburg and might be something important, and because it was the governor, for whom the postmaster had the highest regard, he'd insisted it be delivered tonight. Well, the man was given a tip and in the crate was the typewriter. Lyu unpacked it immediately and started typing. Papa wanted to have a go too, but he was all at sea; the rest of us tried but were equally bad, except for me, who could type a little – honestly. Then we watched Lyu type. After a while Papa tried again, and when Lyu said he had some talent he was most pleased. Mama was overjoyed and said the typewriter was a thing of such beauty that she'd even forgotten the snake. Velya said, 'What's that piece of junk for?' And Katya said she didn't see the point in it: if you had to use your hands you might as well write. But she was overruled.

Are you now *au fait*, my only aunt? It just remains for me to say that the roses are coming into bloom, the cabbage roses and the yellow climbers that have such a peculiar scent, and the wild roses too. The strawberries are ripening and Papa is in the most affable mood. He even asked the other day whether anybody was coming to visit us this summer.

Affectionately, Jessika

Lyu to Konstantin

Kremskoye, 9th June

Dear Konstantin,

Yes, I can sense it: you are my friend. You revere and value in me what we regard to be the higher self, but you know and love my other side too, the ancient flow of ancestral blood, the unfathomable branches of which intervene at every step and cause me to suffer. I shall not hide from you the fact that I am suffering. You realized this some time ago. Perhaps I have never suffered like this before, but I know that it will be overcome. From the very first moment I entered their circle, I have sought to control all these people, and everything else follows from this, for the ruler is bound too, not just the ruled. My successes have become as fateful for me as my failures. I may be able to deceive the governor, but I have no influence over him. This wounds my vanity somewhat, but in the main I lament it for all it gives rise to. The man exudes a kind of magic to which I am not unsusceptible, although it emanates from powers I do not regard as the highest. One can see the characteristics of his lineage, in which the fire of life burns more brightly and beautifully than in common people. There is something perfect about him, though he is certainly not perfect in every way. Indeed, it is his shortcomings that endear him to me; in life's struggle I believe he has grown, become more solid and harder, but he has not extended himself, he has failed to adopt anything new. This is narrow-minded, but it lends him a certain intensity. He has not lost anything either; he retains much of the folly, stubbornness and sincerity of childhood, which those who adapt to new and unfamiliar things usually let go. His ego is whole, so succulent, concentrated and proud that it is painful to touch, and because it is so, I must destroy him. Once I clung to the hope that I could win him over, could open his eyes to other viewpoints. I didn't write to you about my plan; it was far too close to my heart and I already suspected that it would be in vain. My God, this man, this scorching, blind sun! Like a comet I shoot along beside him, and he has no idea that the moment at which our paths meet will tear him into pieces! Let me say nothing of the children. It would have been better, far better, had I exerted the same influence on their father as I have on them. This sounds foolish; after all, it is obvious that young people are easier to influence and control than older ones. But, just once, could not the reverse be true, by chance or miracle? As this is not the case I am trying to reflect on the fact that I have no choice, that I must do what I have acknowledged to be necessary, that the curative power of youth is effusive, that perhaps it is useful to these frolicking children to be jolted by fate. Good God, what does useful mean? In their dream life they were such wonderful souls! It has to end at some point, of course. Children with wrinkles and crooked backs are a perversion and in due course their transition must begin. Perhaps I can even be of assistance to them as they change. Everything a person can want is possible, just so long as there is audacity in the wanting of it.

I shall not write to you again in this vein, and I am also counting on the fact that you will not misconstrue what I say. There is not an ounce of doubt within me. Do not respond to any of this! No words can afford me comfort, and I know that you understand me.

Lyu

Velya to Peter

Kremskoye, 11th June

Dear Peter,

If you wish to experience a moment of history, ensure that you're at home tomorrow or the day after. Our Ivan plunged into a ditch with the motorcar, which he's blaming on the perfidy of the vehicle and we're blaming on the schnapps. As he lay in the ditch for several hours beside the motorcar, he was fairly sober when he returned home, and so the question remains unresolved. The motorcar has suffered more than he; it looks like a tortoise without its shell, but it can still drive. Mama was pleased with the outcome and said we ought to leave it until Ivan could handle the car properly, so he didn't drive us into a ditch too. Papa, on the other hand, said that he couldn't allow the motorcar on the road in that state. Even if it were only Ivan inside, it would damage his reputation; it would be like letting his daughters out with ripped clothes. Persuaded by his argument, we decided that the motorcar must be repaired; Lyu offered to drive the wreck into town and make all the necessary arrangements. Jessika was keen to go with him, but Lyu said no, as given the damage to the vehicle it would not be safe. Since then she has been wandering around looking sorry for herself, for naturally she is in love with Lyu. I say 'naturally' because all women must fall in love with a man like Lyu, whose willpower radiates from every atom of his material being. It's all one to me; even when I'm in love, deep down I don't really care whether I get the woman or not.

For some women this, too, has a certain charm, but it is the will which is truly irresistible. Nobody can fight it; it is the gravity of the soul. Lyu has an active volition with regard to everything. I could not put up with even a year of living like that, yet he has been doing it for twenty-eight years, and will probably grow very old. I doubt whether in the long term he can remain interested in individual women; he ought to be introduced to polygamy. He would not concern himself much with them, but they would be content to suckle for weeks on any phrase he came out with. He will be paying a visit to your mother, so take a good look at him.

Velya

Lyu to Konstantin

Kremskoye, 11th June

Dear Konstantin,

I shall come to Petersburg tomorrow or the day after, and I'm counting on meeting up with you. I need to have the typewriter adapted, and would rather speak to you about this face to face. It can be fitted with an explosive or loaded with a pistol shot. If the latter, however, we could not be sure that the bullet would hit its target. I will soon send it back to the factory from where it was purchased, claiming that it needs to be repaired. It must go there and be sent back in a way that leaves no trace pointing to me in any later investigation. It is your duty to ensure that it doesn't leave without being adapted to our purposes, which means you will need to call on the services of a factory or railway employee. There is no hurry; you can take your time to consider all precautionary measures.

Lyu

Jessika to Tatyana

Kremskoye, 12th June

Dearest Auntie,

I really wanted to visit you, but I may not! I would have loved to have driven past in the crumpled motorcar, precisely because it's so damaged. Just imagine: I would have made myself as pretty as possible and then climbed out of the wrecked shell like a dryad from a hollow trunk. And most importantly of all, I would have seen you, I would have steeled myself for the difficult task of marvelling in envy at your glowing cheeks, at your skin powdered with the lustre of eternal youth. I fear my cheeks are pale and tear-stained at the moment; that's how disappointed I am that I can't go with Lyu.

We shall now be without our protector, Auntie. I suggested the three of us play tag day and night around the house; nobody would be able to creep in unnoticed then. Good old Velya was prepared to play, but not Katya. She said she isn't a child any more. Lyu will bring you this letter. Let him protect you, too, in the meantime, even if you don't need it.

Yours, Jessika

VELYA TO PETER

Kremskoye, 14th June

If I'm not especially active at the moment, the basic reason is that my family always invites contemplation. Adjusting to the colourful circumstances has given rise to my introspection. If I were to get involved it would be bedlam. All hell has broken loose again today. Still exhausted from yesterday – since Lyu has left I have to keep watch until midnight every day, for Mama senses danger – I was sitting in the library, leafing through a book, when Katya flew in like a shuttlecock and rushed to the telephone. To avoid your brain suffering the same shock that mine did at witnessing this scene, I shall offer by way of an explanation that Katya had just told Jessika she was writing a letter to Lyu, and that Jessika, confronted by Katya, blurted out that she loved Lyu and was as good as engaged to him. All this I had to infer, something I should not like to overtax your whale brain with.

So, Katya establishes a connection to Petersburg. I ask her who she wants to speak to. Lyu, even though it's none of my business. I say, 'You could just as easily wait until he returns. It cannot be that important.' Katya: 'How can you be the judge of that? I shall never speak another word to him again here, and I regret ever having done so.' Me: 'Goodness gracious!' At that moment the telephone rings. Katya picks up. 'Is that you? Quack, quack, quack… I just want to let you know how much I loathe you! Quack, quack… You are spineless, a hypocrite, a Judas! Quack, quack, quack, quack. Please don't deny it! You have the nerve to defend yourself? You've deceived me enough already! I am going to tell Jessika everything. Although she's weak, she's too good for a wretch like you. Quack, quack, quack, quack, quack… You think I'm more stupid than I am. You think you're the only clever one and everybody else is a fool, but perhaps it's the other way around!'

Katya blurted all of this out in such a shrill voice that Papa and Mama heard her. Thinking that something had happened, they hurried in. The two of them listened in astonishment and said, 'What is the meaning of this? Who on earth is she talking to?' Me: 'Oh, it's Lyu. She's a tad angry with him.' Katya on the telephone: 'You want me to use the familiar form when addressing you? Such a sly, duplicitous character as you? Never!' Papa and Mama: 'But for goodness' sake, what has he done?' Me: 'Oh, she got a card from him addressed to Katinka von Rasimkara, and she's taken it as an insult to have her name Katya understood as a derivative of Katinka.' Papa and Mama: 'Typical Katya!' The two of them are about to split their sides laughing. Katya turns around. Me: 'Calm down, my little dove!' Katya, casting me a withering look: 'Idiot!' Then she puts the phone down.

I race to the phone and just catch Lyu. I promise to calm things down. With a sigh that stirs my heart even down the telephone he replies, 'You are the oil on the stormy waves of your family. Without you everyone would be seasick.' The conversation appears to have affected him greatly.

I have no idea whether he was speaking from your house, but it would be highly amusing if you'd heard the other half of the conversation. One thing's for sure:

Katya is finished with Lyu, however much her anger may diminish over time. But at this point it's impossible to tell whether she'll dote on your stupidity again after her abortive flirtation with intelligence; at all events don't go counting on it. Besides, she's thriving in her disappointment. My only regret is for poor Jessika. She seems to me like a little bird whose nest has been destroyed, who endures the storm and rain, cautiously chirping in terror and occasionally sticking out her ruffled head to see whether things are getting any better. I think she wept for hours at first; her face trembled for a long while afterwards. There is something about her that is as sweet as an overripe fig, and as soft as a snowflake that melts in your hand. For Jessika it would be a good thing if you married her, but it happened to be Katya who caught your eye first and, according to the law of torpidity that governs you, you stick with her through thick and thin and call this moral fibre. Come on, who you end up caring for should be of no importance to you, but it would be a good thing for Jessika if she were shielded from the world by your thick, saurian skin, whereas Katya has no need of such antediluvian protection; indeed, she might not even be able to put up with it in the long run. But I do not wish to be so foolhardy as to preach sense to someone who has none.

Katya has sufficient discretion to conceal the true state of affairs from Papa and Mama. But whenever

Papa teases her by calling her Katinka, she flashes angry looks at me, which makes everyone else laugh.

Farewell, Velya

LYU TO KONSTANTIN

Kremskoye, 17th June

Dear Konstantin,

It was highly advantageous that I convinced Madame Tatyana to accompany me back to Kremskoye. The influence I wield over her has made an impression on the governor and his family, because they admire greatly this relative of theirs, who plays a significant role in society. She is a beautiful woman and has sufficient presence of mind to know just how much a lady ought to let this show. She has a good, if not educated brain. She likes those intellectual pleasures one can enjoy without too much effort, which is why she prefers the company of knowledgeable, thinking people who are able to clothe her own contemplations in an inspiring form. Her open-mindedness would be more estimable if she were risking anything with such a stance, but this wholly apolitical woman has the freedom to colour her social drabness with naive candour.

Her son, Peter, who has been in love with Katya since childhood and persists with his feelings, unperturbed by the fact that she fails to reciprocate his affection, has, on the surface, something about him of the good-natured giant from fairy tales. With a sort of childish humanity and simplistic sense of justice, he counts himself as a member of the revolutionary party. Although he is envious, because his cousin prefers me to him, he welcomed me, if not with total warmth, then at least with a fair degree of tolerance. Together with some other students, who like him have substantial means at their disposal, he has arranged private courses to allow them to continue their medical studies. Naturally, this is also a protest against the government restrictions. Katya wishes to participate in these courses, which will begin in the near future. The governor knew nothing about this till now; he is deeply shocked that such an initiative should have come from his nephew, and even more so that Katya should wish to take part. As he finds it difficult to be strict with Katya, he began by reproaching his sister, Tatyana, for not preventing her son from undertaking such bothersome, quixotic activities. Smiling like a child, she said her son was now grown up; she could not keep him tied to her apron strings for ever. In any case, Yegor should not bother her with political matters, from which, after all, women were excluded. Why should she form a judgement, the implications of which she could not put into practice? Particularly in society, discussions of political affairs ought to be forbidden, for they immediately turned even the cleverest man into a narrow-minded, bristly ass. Besides, she added, she regarded it absolutely permissible for a young man to take all necessary steps for obtaining the education for his profession if the state deprived him of the means of doing so. After all, a man must have an occupation at some point.

Katya chimed in, insisting how outrageous it was to close the colleges. What was the government thinking of? The universities were independent bodies; ought parents ask the Tsar for permission to allow their children to read and write too?

The governor said that if the university had restricted itself to imparting knowledge the government would have respected it, but by interfering in public affairs and taking sides, it had forfeited its right to inviolability. The hardship brought about by the closure would not be relieved by the fact that those whose fortunes allowed it were obtaining tuition privately; for those without means, the termination of teaching was far more damaging. Then Katya hit back: 'You don't know Peter at all! He's not securing himself advantages over poorer people! It was chiefly to help those without means that he arranged the courses! Everyone can take part, even those who cannot pay!' The governor turned a deep shade of red and said that the situation was worse than he had imagined. It had been his belief that Peter's initiative was no more than private tuition, but this was a rival university, a challenge, a revolutionary act. He'd never have thought it possible that his own child would join the ranks of his opponents.

I have never seen him so incensed. His brow knitted tightly, his nose appeared to blaze, like a freshly sharpened dagger. Around him the atmosphere was eerie, as when a hailstorm is brewing. Katya was a little frightened, but held her ground bravely. With her air of impartiality and her childish smile, Tatyana continued to wonder at how seriously he was regarding the whole affair. Mrs von Rasimkara looked sad. I do not know what she was thinking, but I believe she was the only one other than myself who had a feeling of inevitable doom. Not for any particular reason, only because she loves him and those who love feel fear and suspicion.

In this most unpleasant of moments I put it to the governor that he might send Velya and Katya abroad – he had intended anyway that they should spend some time at foreign universities – then they would no longer create any bother for him here. This suggestion brightened the stormy mood. Velya was enthralled. 'Yes, Papa,' he said, 'all young people from noble families are sent abroad. You must do this too, if you want anything to become of us. I'm all for Paris.' Madame Tatyana said, 'I'll give you Peter, so there's a sensible head amongst you. And Peter needs a sojourn in Paris; he lacks grace.' The governor limited his opposition to saying that he felt Berlin was more appropriate than

Paris, but he was visibly enthused by the idea, and I am convinced that it will come to fruition. I made the suggestion so that Katya and Velya will be away when the misfortune occurs; I will also find a pretext for ensuring that Jessika is not here. Now I think the matter will proceed quickly.

Lyu

KATYA TO VELYA

Petersburg, 20th June

You really are a nincompoop, Velya! In your letter to Peter you told him about the whole story with Lyu! I thought you might, but why are you bragging that you haven't let slip a word of the matter to a single soul? First, I didn't ask you to do it, and second, I didn't believe you for a minute. Now Peter thinks he has to comfort me and I have to marry him; he is not a logical individual. And sadly, he's charming about my not being in love with him. Now I have to put up with this silliness from Peter while listening to Aunt Tatyana wax lyrical about Lyu: how elegant he is, how inspiring, how energetic, and what a great influence he's had on us! Look after Jessika at least! It's too bad that she's got such parents. Papa takes notice of nothing, Mama likes everything and you don't care about anything.

Just remember you're a man. Lyu can do what he likes with you and make you believe anything, as if you were in love with him. That's ignoble of you. When Aunt Tatyana isn't talking about Lyu, she's delightful and very sensible. The courses have not yet begun. What's happening about Paris? Has Papa said yes? If needs be we'll go to Berlin too, of course. Once we're abroad the rest will fall into place.

Adieu, Katya

JESSIKA TO KATYA

Kremskoye, 20th June

My sweet little ladybird,

I'd rather weep than write to you, but then you'd know nothing of what's going on. I cannot rid myself of the feeling that it's my fault you've gone away. In any case, I'm certain that I'm to blame for something, and it all started when I wrote to Lyu. You cannot deny that you were livid. To begin with I thought that you were in love with Lyu too, but he laughed and said you most certainly weren't, and when I saw you together afterwards, I no longer thought you were. And if you did love him, you certainly didn't love him in the way I did; you wouldn't die if he didn't love you back. But that's how I felt. You're not the type to fall in love so seriously, are you, my little mouse? After all, Velya keeps saying you're not as sentimental as I am. Write something of comfort to me! Everyone here is unhappy now. Papa has been terribly nervous since you left, visitors strain his nerves, but I believe it's mainly on account of your courses. It's disastrous for him if his daughter and nephew are involved in something that's directed against the government. Yesterday a few library books were discovered, which Velya had borrowed a year or two ago and forgotten to return. As the cost on these is quite considerable, Papa was furious and made a hell of a row. He said Velya was careless and profligate, behaving as if he were a millionaire. He'd reduce the whole lot of us to poverty. When Mama, who arrived on the scene, tried to defend Velya, Papa really flew into a rage. When we sat down for lunch everyone was serious and quiet, Papa staring sombrely into the distance. Mama picked up her lorgnette, looked from one person to the next in puzzlement, then finally stared at Papa for a while and asked tenderly, 'Why are you so pale, Yegor?' We all started laughing, including Papa, which lightened the mood.

Velya was mainly disconsolate because one of the things Papa said was that he was too reckless to be sent away on a long trip. But he only said this in anger; I think he'll allow the two of you to go.

Is Peter torturing you terribly? Don't worry about me. Lyu told me from the outset that he couldn't and wouldn't propose to me until he'd found a suitable position. He said he just wanted to be my friend; you can see how honourable he is. Velya would never be like that. My dearest ladybird, I miss you hourly. Don't you miss me too?

Affectionately, Jessika

LUSINYA TO KATYA

Kremskoye, 21st June

My dear little Katya,

Well, now you've got your way. Are you glad to be in the city? Does it make you smarter, better, happier? I do not intend to hide from you, my darling, that your leaving here, even though you could see what you were doing to Papa, was painful for me. Is that so difficult to comprehend? For if you had understood this correctly, you could not have done it. What hurts him most is not that you think differently, nor that you're acting against his wishes. But his love for you is too great to forbid you what he would forbid others. He loves you in spite of the fact that you're doing something that, were anybody else to do it, they would forfeit his sympathy at a stroke. He's driving himself mad, his system is driving him mad, everything is driving him mad. Why are you inflicting this on your father, an ageing man who adores you? Are you achieving something of significance for yourself or others? Listen, I sometimes think that our children exist to exact revenge on us, and yet I couldn't say for whom or for what. Children are the only beings towards whom we are utterly selfless, which is why they're the only ones who can truly destroy us. In a few years' time, perhaps, you will be a mother yourself. Then you will understand me and also know that I can make such observations without my love for you being diminished in the slightest.

I think in the end that Papa will send you and Velya abroad; he's already keen on the idea, and it would be the best thing for all of us. Lyu is a support for us at the moment. I owe him my gratitude and yet I would prefer it if we, your father and I, were completely alone after your departure. The holiday has not yet benefited him in the way that I'd hoped for, perhaps on account of the excessive commotion and unrest there has been around us. For the time being I am not afraid for him, as I am too full of things which are worse than physical dangers.

Please be considerate towards Aunt Tatyana, my darling, and also towards Peter. I will not force you to marry a man you do not love, but seek to preserve the friendship of a good man.

Lovingly, Mama

Velya to Katya

Kremskoye, 23rd June

God knows how, but your bird brain came up with a good idea when you decided to leave. Birds and mice can sense when food is scarce, that's instinct, and I will not deny you that. It is, in fact, very uncomfortable here. Yesterday morning Mama found another threatening letter beneath her pillow, saying that if Demodov and the other students are not pardoned, Papa will follow or precede them to the grave. This would be the final warning he would receive. That same day a letter arrived by post from Demodov's mother, in which she pleaded with him to spare her son's life. Is there any connection with the written threat? Mama found the content of the letter less shocking than the fact that she didn't discover it until the morning and thus had lain on it all night long; she finds that sinister. What is really strange is how it got there. None of our people could have been involved; it's out of the question. Who else can gain access to Mama and Papa's bedroom? Obviously there must be a natural explanation, but we cannot get to the bottom of the matter. They're saying that somebody must have climbed through the window late at night. This seems rather unlikely to me, but of course I cannot disprove it either. Lyu is deeply embarrassed because his protection has shown itself so clearly to be inadequate. It's my belief that he hasn't really been thinking about it recently. Today we had a long conversation about the affair. He takes it for granted that the writer of this threatening letter knew of the letter Mrs Demodov wrote, and hence must be from Demodov's circle of friends. Of course, there is no reason to think that Mrs Demodov knows any of this. Lyu says that, in all probability, the sole purpose of the letter is to elicit a favourable reply to Mrs Demodov's plea, to enhance its impact, so to speak. But it will fail in its goal, of course, given Papa's character. Lyu said he respects and loves Papa, who always acts according to his character and reason, but it had to be admitted that the revolution was right and he was wrong. The government, he continued, had decided to arrest a universally respected professor, one of the few with the courage to express his opinions, and send him to Siberia; Demodov wanted to defend him and the rights of the university. In the future this handful of students would be highlighted as proof of the fact that there had been young men of courage and honour in Petersburg at the time. In this case, Lyu argued, essentially the government was the agitator and lawless barbarian, whereas the so-called revolutionaries were the guardians of justice. In informing Papa of their views and intentions, and giving him the time to choose another course that would be acceptable to them, they were acting with decency. Naturally, I agreed with him, but I said I could empathize with Papa for refusing to give in now. Maybe, Lyu said, if Papa knew for certain that the threats were meant seriously and would be acted upon, he would do it out of love for his wife and children. But I don't believe this, and one would not be able to persuade him to change his mind at any rate. Papa is the only one who is quite unruffled; I love this about him. There is not even a shadow of fear about him. It might still have been possible earlier, but there is no way he will back down now. Naturally, defiance, obstinacy and cantankerousness play their part too, but it is a noble stance all the same. Mama is sad. She, of course, thinks it's terrible that the students will be executed, or at least Demodov will, and that Papa could change this but won't. But I believe the reason why she hasn't tried to appeal to him again is that she knows it would be fruitless. Both Papa and Mama are people of extraordinary taste; I wouldn't have chosen any other parents for me, even though their personalities and views are often quite strange.

Lyu also said that, in his opinion, Papa's life was not currently in danger; the situation will perhaps only become critical when sentence is actually passed on the students. Our servants are utterly loyal, he added, and that's why we shouldn't be too worried about Papa. I had asked him about this because he was so unusually serious and pensive. He said he'd realized he would have to leave us as soon as possible and this made him sad.

He would have left anyway, but now he was bringing the date forward. The discrepancy between his ideas and Papa's was too great, he said, and thus he could not regard their cooperation as seemly. I've tried to dissuade him.

At any rate I'm staying here to provide a little distraction for Mama and Papa; I feel sorry for them. Jessika is just in love. Thank goodness I am not; it's a ghastly way to be. Behave decently, darling, to spare Papa any inconveniences at this time.

Velya

Yegor von Rasimkara to Mrs Demodov
Kremskoye, 23rd June

Dear Madam,

If your son had insulted or attacked me personally, it would not have required your intercession for me to forgive unconditionally the offence on account of his youth and impetuosity. Regrettably, it is not a private individual you have appealed to, but a representative of the government, and as such I cannot be magnanimous, for when it comes to the state what counts are not feelings, but utility and necessity. For his benefit as well as that of his parents, I gave the young man, whose views were known to me, sufficient warning.

By ignoring my warning, he declared his intention to accept the consequences of his actions. I trust that he himself will neither beg for mercy nor reproach the government for its severity.

Only if I were able to grant your plea, Madam, would I perhaps have the right to tell you how much I sympathize with your situation. Please allow me nevertheless to tell you that I would be very grateful for the opportunity to prove my genuine and painful compassion in deed.

Yours faithfully, Yegor von Rasimkara

LYU TO KONSTANTIN

Kremskoye, 24th June

Dear Konstantin,

The letter I placed beneath Mrs von Rasimkara's pillow affected her greatly. She did not find it until the morning, having slept on it all night. This is what unsettles her most, as well as the question of how the letter got there in the first place. And yet she is composed; she is convinced that her husband is doomed, that nobody can alter his fate, and now she is waiting for the inevitable to occur. But this is a disposition that can be banished by other dispositions, or it is a fundamental awareness over which the day surges time and again.

The governor is almost impervious to the shocking, and moreover inexplicable, incident. Without delay he gave a negative response to Mrs Demodov's plea. I cannot detect a change in him, but he has been suffering for some time on account of his daughter Katya's behaviour. He does not seem to think it possible that he might be in serious danger; at any rate he does not wish to think it possible.

I predicted that it would come to this. I would have gladly saved this unflinching, imperturbable man; for too long, perhaps, I entertained the possibility that I could do so. If I have suffered from hubris, I may be cured of this by the experiences I have amassed in this house. I realize that only God can change a man, or not even God! This could console my pride. We have as little power over people as we do over the stars; we see them rise and set according to their engrained laws. It will not be much longer now; there is no way out. I myself would prefer it to be over soon.

KATYA TO VELYA

Petersburg, 25th June

Velya, I don't believe you've ever been fully awake since you were born. Please finally wake up! I am being criticized from all sides. I can accept this from others, but from you? Outrageous! What am I doing wrong? Papa has his ideas and I have mine. Why does he have a greater right to live by his than I do? His are more damaging than mine, I believe. After all, I'm not killing anybody. Because he is older than me, perhaps? A fine reason: at most his age counts against him. But I certainly love him as much as you do, probably more than you. You don't even understand that Lyu cannot remain in the house if he holds the sorts of views he expressed to you. We may believe that Papa is wrong, and that ultimately we cannot blame the opposing party if they kill him, but this is very different from a stranger articulating the same thoughts. What do we actually know about Lyu? I know that he is completely unscrupulous. This naturally impresses you; it impressed me to begin with too. It may even be estimable – perhaps you lack scruples as well, perhaps I may have as few as he – but it's all the same to me: he must not stay in our house any longer. Can you not see that he would be quite happy to have father killed? At least keep your eyes open and watch out! I felt greatly unnerved when I read your letter. He fixes his icy eyes on Papa and thinks: they would actually be in the right if they were to kill you. Why is he there at all? Surely you realize that he's not the right man for Jessika. Besides, he doesn't even want to marry her; he's only making her unhappy. Mama must understand the story with Jessika too, and of course she mustn't know about the other thing so she doesn't start worrying. Now listen to me: you mustn't hold him back; on the contrary, you have to say, 'Yes, go at once. You ought to have done it long ago!' If you were a man you'd have already told him that he needs to leave the house for Jessika's sake. Be a man for once! Unfortunately Papa sees and hears nothing; it would actually be better if in his professional life he played the role he plays at home, and vice versa, for then both the family and the people would be content. Poor man, he sacrifices himself to his inflated sense of duty – and yet there's something beautiful about such ridiculousness. I don't know which I like better, this or Lyu's unscrupulousness. Oh well, Papa is Papa and that is why he acts as he does. We must watch over him and you must vouch for him, do you hear?

Katya

LUSINYA TO TATYANA

Kremskoye, 26th June

Dear Tatyana,

It is as if you took the sun away with you; we've only had horrible rainy days since. That day you arrived was such a surprise, and how carefree and bright it was! We won't have another one like that for a long time. When we moved out here in May, I thought only of the time before me, which I imagined would be indescribably happy, having Yegor all to myself, far away from business and worries. I felt as if there would be nothing to follow this. I expect one always feels like this when anticipating such a happy time; happiness seems eternal although, on the contrary, it can only be fleeing. Now I realize that the summer will pass and that, even before it's over, the time will come when we must return to the city and the trial will start, with all its attendant horrors for us and others.

Yegor will not escape the mass and energy of the hatred that has accumulated towards him. If only they knew the man! But they know only his deeds. And is the man not measured by his deeds? O God, I promised myself that I wouldn't judge. There is so much to weigh up on both sides that I could easily be wrong. Only – and this I know for certain – Yegor would never act out of innate cruelty or a thirst for revenge; he has always believed he is doing the right thing, and it has often been difficult for him. Maybe he's wrong, but the fact that he can be mistaken makes him no less dear to me. He places the highest value on the prevailing order and legitimate power. My inclinations would have taken me in a different direction, but that makes me no better than him. It's in the blood: he inherited different blood from his ancestors than I did from mine.

O Tatyana, I have a heavy heart! Wherever I look, all is dark, so uniformly dark that it has already occurred to me that it may be my eyes which can no longer see the light. But tell me, where can I find something good, some comfort? How will the conflict with the children end? They are merely following their inclinations, proud that they are barely paying attention to us. Do all people have to experience this? Well, perhaps we made our parents experience something similar, but that doesn't make this any less bitter.

Fear is the worst. I think that fear has unnerved me so much that I can no longer take pleasure in anything, nor can I even summon any from myself. I am permanently afraid, day and night, even when I'm asleep. That is the worst. I bet you cannot imagine how it is to sleep and dream, all the while being tortured by fear. Ever since I found that letter beneath my pillow I feel like someone condemned to death who doesn't know when the sentence will be carried out. The murderer must have come through the open window, you see, having crept up the outside of the house like a snake. He must have stood beside my bed, very close, and slipped the letter under the pillow. He must have arrived silently, really like a snake; you remember, don't you, that when Lyu came into our room that time I woke immediately. I expect the man was holding a knife or a rope and could have murdered Yegor on the spot, but he wanted to give him a deadline, or at that moment he didn't have the heart to do it, or he just wanted to keep us on tenterhooks. Every successive night could be the one when he returns to carry out the deed.

And why didn't Lyu hear anything? Well, why should he have heard any more than we did, given that it all happened right next to us? In the face of this catastrophe even his vigilance is ineffective. He seems to be quite a changed man since that night, serious and withdrawn, but these words fail to describe adequately his character. I am certain he is suffering from not being able to achieve what he had promised and what I believed him capable of. It must disturb him deeply. He can see that we are a lost cause. He does not want to be present. Or what if he cannot protect us because he mustn't? Because of the views he holds. Has he perhaps seen and recognized those who are hunting Yegor? Has he recognized friends amongst them? Or some people he deems to be more important than us? This suspicion – no, not a suspicion, a train of thought – will seem like madness to you. It would never have occurred to me if I didn't have his strange presence before my eyes. There is something mysterious about him. Occasionally, when his gaze alights on Yegor and myself, I feel a shudder. I have nothing to reproach him for; the sympathy I feel for the man speaks volumes for him. If it is true that he could protect us and yet doesn't think he should, then he believes himself to be right. O God, everybody is right, all those who hate and kill and malign others – O God, what a world we live in! What convolution! In the end the victor will be the one for whom it is disentangled.

I admit that my nerves are overwrought. In these circumstances it is excusable, don't you think, Tatyana? Yegor is completely without fear. I love him so much; I believe I have never loved him as I do now. That is happiness too. I know that I am happy compared to many, many other women; but a black curtain hangs before this knowledge. Will a good wind come along and tear it away? Think of me, darling.

Yours, Lusinya

Velya to Katya

Kremskoye, 27th June

Katinka, my little dove, what nonsense are you writing about my sleeping and waking? And about Lyu's unscrupulousness and Papa's sense of duty, which impress you in turns? Father, Thy will be done! If you had a keen psychological eye, you would have noticed that Lyu is a theoretician; it is not his inclination to act. He thinks that certain people would be in the right if they killed Papa. Is this new? Of course they would be in the right. When they planned to blow up the Tsar last year we were also agreed that they were in the right, and yet they didn't carry it out. Which means you could also think me possible of killing Father. One doesn't do something like that even though one may think it an excellent idea in theory or endorse it; as a civilized being one is prevented from doing it. The simple fact of the matter is that you're still jealous. I'd have thought better of you. Love makes all women stupid and petty. I grant it would be better for Jessika's sake if Lyu were to leave. I like only to be in love myself; in others I cannot stand it as it makes them ridiculous. For Jessika it has become an affliction. That means I can imagine that other people find it delightful; even I sometimes feel it is like a blossoming cherry tree in flames. A beautiful thing in itself, but when I think that she is a human being and my sister, I find it silly. I also told Lyu that the matter has run its course and it would be good if it now came to an end. He was in complete agreement and said he'd long been toying with the idea of leaving our house; he just wanted to be sure that Mama was happy for him to go. You can see how wrong you are. Perhaps he will accompany us abroad; that will only work of course if you behave sensibly. He cannot marry every woman who falls in love with him, you silly thing! Would I have done that? As far as you're concerned there's absolutely no need for you to marry. You're a frightfully sweet darling, but you'd be ridiculous as a wife and mother.

Velya

Lyu to Konstantin

Kremskoye, 29th June

Dear Konstantin,

I have asked Mrs von Rasimkara to release me. I told her that the episode with the letter had convinced me that my presence here was useless. I had been racking my brains day and night, trying to establish how it could have happened, but had arrived at no conclusion. Nobody could have come through the window, I said, for I would have heard it. In my opinion the servants were above suspicion; I regarded them as unswervingly loyal. She interrupted me, saying animatedly that on this point she had no doubts. I said the only possibility was that a servant could have done it under hypnosis. Even so, this was improbable. She was greatly interested in this idea and we discussed it for a while. In any case, she said, she wanted to let the matter with the letter rest; nothing would come of it. Her husband had no intention of starting an actual investigation; he tended to ignore threatening letters, attaching little importance to them. Till now, she added, events had proved him right. I neither disputed this nor agreed with her. At any rate, I said, the situation had reached the point where she no longer needed me, whether this was because there was no danger or because I could not guarantee that I would be capable of averting it.

She asked me where I was thinking of going and what I was planning to do. I said I wished to complete my work; this was the most important thing as far as I was concerned. If I made peace with my father I would stay at home for the time being; he had recently written me a conciliatory letter. Otherwise I would find refuge with a friend. She said that she and her husband owed me their gratitude and that I must permit them to assist me if I needed help. This would not be a good deed, but the repayment of a debt. She was earnest, gracious, so incredibly refined. If it suited me, she said, I was free to go immediately, but if I were unsure about my next move, I should stay as long as I liked. I said I wanted to try to come to an understanding with my father and I would be grateful to her if I could take advantage of her hospitality for another fortnight; the matter would be resolved by then. I wanted to kiss her hand, which is very beautiful, but then remembered what I am intending to do to her, so left it.

My impression was that she was pleased by my announcement, for Jessika's sake, I expect. I even believe she thinks that it is on account of Jessika that I consider it my duty to leave, and this is why she feels such gratitude towards me. Farewell!

Lyu

JESSIKA TO TATYANA

Kremskoye, 29th June

Dearest, loveliest Auntie,

I think I shall come to visit you soon. The few days that you spent here were so wonderful! Your presence made everyone cheerful and relaxed. Now things are dreadful. Lyu is going to leave us. He says he has to go because his being here has shown itself to be unnecessary and because Mama no longer needs him. To begin with, of course, Mama said she'd never felt as safe and secure as now because Lyu was here. But Papa never liked the arrangement, and he will have told Mama that he no longer wanted it. You know that Papa doesn't like having strangers around him; even when you were here it affected his nerves. Deep down Mama is certainly sad that Lyu is leaving. And if Velya and Katya go as well! Papa is almost convinced that the best plan would be for them to go to university in Berlin or Paris. Velya is very excited and, of course, Katya is too. I don't begrudge them it; they love to travel. But then, Aunt Tatyana, please let me stay with you until we move back to the city. Being here on my own is too sad, after such a delightful May. The atmosphere is so stifling. Papa and Mama will agree to it; perhaps it will do them some good to be alone together. Papa will have the best opportunity to relax and the servants will comfortably be able to look after just the two of them without my help. Lyu doesn't know where he's going. He told me that if he were to go to Petersburg he would pay you a visit if you would allow. He often raves about your beauty and your mind. Who wouldn't? Especially

your little Jessika

VELYA TO KATYA

Kremskoye, 1st July

Well, my sweet little sparrow, is your crest all ruffled in anger at your brother because he told you the truth, as is his duty? In the meantime he is working for your, his and all of our benefit. Ever since Papa persuaded himself that we can only obtain a weightier education if we spend a few terms studying in the cultured West, his mood has greatly improved again. He too now thinks it a good idea for us to begin in the more superficial Paris, then progress to the rigorously philosophical Germany. We are to leave soon, for Papa was struck by the sudden realization that all our shortcomings were exclusively a result of our not having experienced the old Western culture. You must, therefore, abandon your studies at once and sort out our effects, which is to say watch while Aunt Tatyana does it.

Lyu is leaving, maybe before we do. I think he'll come to Paris too, if we're there, although he has not said anything definite about this yet. We often take a drive together in the motorcar. I had to promise Mama that I'd leave him alone with Jessika as seldom as possible, a totally redundant commitment as he has no desire for that anyway. I'm also being terribly considerate of Papa; I don't play Wagner any more, because it makes him nervous. He's really much better now, by the way. Besides his old typewriter he has our trip to keep him happily occupied. He gives me instructions as to which trains we must take, which hotels we ought to stay in, and almost feels as if he could come along too. Be grateful to your brother rather than sulking, which is utterly childish.

Velya

VELYA TO PETER

Kremskoye, 1st July

Dear Peter,

The best thing would be for you to come to Paris with us. My mother, who is also in favour of our going, wants you to accompany us, for she regards you as more sensible than Katya and me. You only need promise me that you'll refrain from any love-struck nonsense with Katya. But you're not like that. What you actually feel inside is obviously none of my business. If your departure puts an end to your courses, then so much the better. Papa has enough trouble as it is; it's not hard to feel terribly sorry for him. We can return to formulating our ideas when we're back. For my part I'd be very glad of a break. In Paris you will develop politically too; I can already see you as a mature Robespierre bursting into Russia.

Yours, Velya

LUSINYA TO KATYA

Kremskoye, 2nd July

My dearest child,

It has been decided that you and Velya will go to Paris. You're excited, aren't you? I think you will be sensible and not spend too much money. After all, you're old enough to understand our circumstances and behave accordingly. You have the best father, who has never tried to get rich illegitimately, or even in an ungentlemanly way, as so many do. For this reason I hope you respect and love him all the more, and you are proud of the relative modesty of our means. Notwithstanding, he has always provided for you with extravagant kindness; do not abuse his generosity. Overstepping the mark would not only cause him worry, but be seriously unpleasant for him. Within this limit, my darling, you should heartily enjoy your freedom and use the means put at your disposal to turn yourselves into whole individuals.

I think that once you two and Lyu have left, Jessika will go to stay with Aunt Tatyana. A good deal more suffering still lies in store for her tender heart. She will suffer less there than here, so I shall not stand in her way. For her sake it's necessary for Lyu to go. I shall miss his stimulating manner of talking, combining obvious ideas with more obscure and interesting ones. He never lets go a word that one utters, but catches and develops it further. I cherish this about him, but most of all that he is a person of substance, a man with an intense awareness of all things and a clear will. On the other hand, his leaving will ease my state of mind, and not only on account of Jessika. For me there is something unfamiliar and inscrutable about him, which at times has perturbed me greatly. He has a peculiar gaze; perhaps this is how he achieved such power over Jessika. The fact is, he does not belong to our family and not even his appreciation for very different people can bridge the gap. And then he sleepwalks, which I cannot come to terms with.

After all the agitation of this summer I am looking forward to being alone with Papa. I really am looking forward to it, so please do not worry on our account. You will write us many lovely letters and we will accompany you in spirit to the *Mona Lisa*, the Place de la Concorde and the fountains of Versailles. It now occurs to me that while we don't even need to put on hats here, you must have travelling clothes and all manner of other things. There is much that you will no doubt be able to purchase more cheaply and tastefully in Paris. If only you were more practical children! Can I leave it to you? In any event, you need to take a few items from here, so attend to this now. You have on hand Aunt Tatyana, the best adviser. Farewell, my darling child. Please write soon to your father to tell him you're looking forward to Paris.

Lovingly, Mama

KATYA TO YEGOR

Petersburg, 4th July

Dear Papa,

It is terribly decent of you to let us go to Paris. But some good will come of it for you too, as you'll be rid of us. Peter might want to come with us, which is fine by me as he is so practical as to be indispensable. For example, he can repair a car, however complicated the problem. This is why Lyu specifically drove into town that time. He replaces a porter, locksmith, decorator, tailor, cook and even cleaning lady – albeit his taste is a little dated. He's now also very discreet towards me. It seems almost as if he were no longer in love, which in fact is a shame, even though I sometimes found it irksome. But I appreciate that it's better for our journey. What's more, he's just as obliging as he ever was; yesterday he bound a book very beautifully for me and made me a key to replace one I'd lost, which Aunt Tatyana mustn't find out about.

If Peter comes with us, we'll save lots of money because he always pays attention to these things. Should I come back again and say adieu? I'd be very happy to do so, but you'd have to send Lyu away first as I cannot abide him and his presence would spoil the occasion for me.

Your littlest one, Katya

LUSINYA TO TATYANA

Kremskoye, 5th July

My dearest Tatyana,

I must tell you that I'm completely over my melancholic mood. There has been a turnaround inside me, because it simply couldn't go on as it was. One often discovers the dullest truisms; in my case it is the old saying that God helps the brave. To begin with, it was a considerable effort for me to suppress my fear and look to the future with confidence, but after having done it a few times, all of a sudden it seemed as if I were being borne along by an unknown force, and I was overflowing with cheerfulness. This is partly because Yegor's good mood has returned ever since he took the decision to allow the children to go to Paris. It causes me such pain to see him so gloomy and helplessly sad. Now I am thoroughly looking forward to the time when we shall be alone. I don't believe we've ever been completely on our own since we've had the children. And in the country, with nothing to do, in such beautiful surroundings! It all needs to happen quickly now, otherwise our holiday will be over before they've all gone. Yegor is looking forward to it too; he just keeps saying that I cannot live for him and him alone, because I am used to giving myself to many people and many things. In his heart of hearts, however, he knows that I'll only be in my element when I'm alone with him. When does one finally get older? Ever since my twentieth birthday I've been getting ever younger – me! This is not true of my hair and skin, of course.

Dear Tatyana, would you help my little Katya obtain what she needs for her journey? You have such good taste and discernment. If your Peter were to accompany them to Paris, it would reassure us greatly. Although he's only just older than Velya, it would be as if they were travelling with a mentor. I first envisaged Lyu in this role, but Katya's aversion to him cannot be overcome. And when I think of how she raved about him to begin with! He was an oracle for all three children. Then on one occasion he called her Katinka instead of Katya and that was that for good. My children appear quite mad at times; God only knows where they get it from. Of course, Tatyana, I don't believe that his using the wrong name is the only reason for her feelings. I imagine that all manner of things have occurred amongst the children, jealousy and suchlike. In character, Lyu and Katya would actually suit each other rather well, at least better than Lyu and Jessika, but opposites tend to attract, don't they? At any rate, Katya's dislike of Lyu is preferable to me than the opposite. I would also be happier if Peter accompanied them. I know that Lyu loves and understands the children. There is something imposing, something versatile about him, and in this respect he would be suited as their leader. But I fancy I'd sometimes be haunted by dreams where he sleepwalks into her bedroom, stands by her bed and gazes at her with that inscrutable look of his.

O Tatyana, there's something I really have to tell you! When I found that threatening letter beneath my pillow, Lyu said that it could have been placed there by someone in the house who'd been hypnotized by someone else; that was a possibility. Then I thought of his inscrutable look and his nocturnal wanderings, and it dawned on me that he himself might have been possessed by an alien, demonic will. At the time the idea was so grim, I wasn't able to discuss it with anyone, nor write to you about it. Now I can happily talk and even laugh about it. I told Yegor recently, who found it so funny that I cannot help laughing when I think of it. He said that the more ludicrous the story, the more willing I was to believe it. But I do not think something like that to be altogether impossible, otherwise why would Lyu have mentioned it?

So are you in favour, dear Tatyana, of Jessika's coming to visit you? If Peter goes abroad you'd be all alone otherwise, and Jessika loves spending time with you. We'd be very happy if she could be of some assistance to you.

JESSIKA TO KATYA

Kremskoye, 8th July

Dear little one,

Do not get angry, but it really is beastly of you to refuse to come while Lyu is here, thereby driving him out of the house. He has not deserved that from us. It is my belief that you think he acted badly towards me, which is not the truth at all. He does love me, but he said at the beginning that he was unsure whether he could ever marry me because he was too proud and that I had to turn my feelings into friendship. Which is exactly what I've done, and what is wrong with his being my friend? After all, he's Velya's friend too, and indeed was yours until you behaved so disgracefully towards him. He can arrange it so he's out all day when you're here.

The affair is embarrassing for Papa and Mama too, and as you have so many lovely things to look forward to, you could be considerate in such small matters.

Are you angry, my little bluebottle, for my saying this? You have to admit I rarely moralize towards you. But I suppose you will do as you please. Papa and Mama are now in very good spirits; it's terribly sweet how they are looking forward to being on their own. They sometimes look like a couple engaged to be married: young, beautiful and mysteriously blessed. I'm delighted that this is rose time; in a few weeks they will all be in bloom and Mama can adorn her table with roses every day, put them in her hair and fill all the vases.

Jessika

VELYA TO PETER

Kremskoye, 10th July

Dear Peter,

Something strange happened to me yesterday. I went to look for Lyu in his room and, as he wasn't there, I waited for him. Sitting down at his desk, I leafed absent-mindedly through his writing case and noticed a piece of paper with some handwriting that caught my eye. I didn't know why, to begin with, but then it struck me that the threatening letter Mama found under her pillow had been written in the same hand, or a very similar one. Just imagine, I got a terrible fright for the first time in my life; everything around me was spinning. I wasn't certain what was actually horrifying me, but in a trice my hands and temples were covered in sweat. My unconscious was probably forming a host of conclusions at lightning speed, the result of which was the horror. I swiftly left the room and tried to collect my thoughts. I swear to you: I was so distraught that I couldn't think clearly. When Lyu came back I arranged it so that we sat in his room, I leafed through his case, fiddled with the piece of paper and then noted casually how the handwriting was similar to that in the threatening letter. 'Indeed,' Lyu said gleefully. 'I too think one could conclude it is the same. I have tried to reproduce it from memory, so it could be used to trace the writer, but your father does not wish for the matter to be pursued.' Papa tore the letter up, you see, which is what he always does with anonymous missives. It is simply unbelievable that this could happen to me! I knew that initially Lyu was toying with the idea of finding out who had written the letter, and also knew that he is very interested in graphology! Anyway, when I heard his voice and saw him, my excitement suddenly felt childish. Afterwards I really wanted to tell Lyu the truth of what had happened, but I couldn't utter the words, I don't know why. He has absolutely no idea and is delighted by his success; after all, it is a colossal achievement to imitate someone's handwriting from memory so deceptively.

I tell myself that the reason for my foolishness is that the episode with the threatening letter did in fact set my nerves on edge. If Papa were a different man, I think one would really be afraid, but he exudes such assurance that it seems impossible anything could happen to him. After all, these sorts of horror stories are what one encounters in potboilers, not in one's own life. Having said that, assassinations do occur from time to time. But Papa said he is not widely hated and the students in question are educated individuals, amongst whom one wouldn't find murderers. It was clear, he said, that the last letter was intended merely to intimidate him. Besides, one could fall ill just like that and die; one was always confronted with death, so these sorts of things merited no attention. Sometimes I wonder whether Papa's fearlessness is an advantage or a flaw; perhaps he just has no imagination.

He is now in a very genial mood. His typewriter has fallen to pieces and he spends hours with Lyu tinkering with it, in an attempt to identify the problem. Lyu approaches the matter enthusiastically and seriously; I cannot work out whether he does this to please Papa or because he really is interested too.

Dear God, I will be happy when we are in Paris. There is nothing I can do here to help or change anything. Don't breathe a word to Katya about my episode with Lyu. Papa says one can travel second class perfectly comfortably in Germany. Thy will be done, Father; now I just want to get going.

Velya

Jessika to Katya

Kremskoye, 14th July

Katya, on no account are you to come, do you hear? I just hope you haven't already left! Look, yesterday the gaffer fell terribly ill. He had cramps, he was twisting and turning and he went blue in the face; it was simply dreadful. First Velya said he was drunk, but we soon could see that it was something different. The maids said he had cholera and made an indescribable fuss; nobody wanted to stay with him. Lyu took everything in hand, he said it couldn't be cholera, as the symptoms were different; it was probably a typhoid fever with some complications. He prescribed all manner of things and stayed with Ivan, even though Papa and Mama were horrified, because they thought it could be infectious. Lyu said that he didn't think this to be the case and, besides, he wasn't worried in the slightest about it, which meant he wasn't susceptible to it. Ivan stared at him in horror when he came to; I think he doesn't like having Lyu near him, though he'd never dare say as much. When the doctor arrived he said that everything Lyu had prescribed was appropriate, he himself wouldn't have acted any differently and he too believed it was typhoid fever. Papa and Mama do not wish you to come under any circumstances, because of the risk of infection. We're here and there's nothing we can do to change that, but you should not wilfully expose yourself to the danger, they say. I think they are absolutely right: there's nothing you can do to help, and Mama would worry, even if the infectiousness is not so bad. For the moment Ivan cannot be transported into town because he is too sick. Poor gaffer! Velya always says it's a pity about him; he really enjoyed his wine and the schnapps made him very happy.

Now it's almost certain I won't see you before you go, my little glow-worm! But I won't be missing you; there's too much to do at the moment!

Yours, Jessika

LYU TO KONSTANTIN

Kremskoye, 16th July

Dear Konstantin,

I have sent off the typewriter. Let us stick to the plan of having the explosion detonated when the Y and shift keys are pressed. As we have to agree on a letter, it ought to be that with which the governor's Christian name begins; it is inconceivable that he could write to anyone without using it. For now the responsibility lies on your shoulders. I am glad to be free from it for a short while, for I feel sick. There is a fever in my bones and I would like nothing better than to retire to bed, but I believe that I can prevent the illness from developing by fighting it. The coachman, Ivan, has a severe case of typhoid and his life is still in danger. As such terror and helplessness reigned here – the servants claimed he had cholera – and I have some knowledge in this area, I attended to him. The man cannot bear me. He feels a vague fear or aversion towards me; he senses, as animals can, the danger I pose to his master. I have a particular fondness for these mentalities that are still semi-animalistic and live in the unconscious. It was a real pleasure for me to treat and observe him. Perhaps I overexerted myself in caring for him, as I was already infected.

Should the illness prove stronger than me and I am brought to hospital in Petersburg, this would be very bad. For I must take receipt of the machine and set it up myself. I can, however, assume with certainty that Mr and Mrs von Rasimkara would keep me in the house and look after me, even if I were to baulk at this. Above all, I am counting on my healthy constitution and the strength of my will. I am sure I can no longer tear down walls like Samson, but I can keep my body upright if it feels like collapsing, for a while longer at least. At all events, please wait for another sign of life from me before you act.

Lyu

LUSINYA TO TATYANA

Kremskoye, 18th July

Dearest Tatyana,

How terribly quickly the countenance of all earthly things can change, indeed more quickly than the overcast sky. This is a platitude that reveals itself to us suddenly like an epiphany when we experience it. Our good old Ivan seems to be in better shape; at least the doctor says that if the illness had progressed to its conclusion, his condition would have worsened substantially. You know how close we feel to our people here; having others would be for us just as sad as moving to another house. Watching a person in mortal danger, watching him virtually die, causes me terrible anguish. Suddenly it becomes clear that this is the fate of all of us, that the shadow of death could have just as easily descended upon me, and perhaps will tomorrow or the day after, but will inevitably descend on me one day. Then I am seized by a fear, a fear that is a thousand times worse than death. Yes, it seems to have passed over Ivan this time. But yesterday evening Lyu had to retire to his bed. He has cared for Ivan so attentively and exposed himself to infection, as if it were the most natural thing in the world. Our admiration for him is all the greater as Ivan has always disliked him and made no secret of this fact. He was already not quite himself the day before yesterday, but when I asked him he claimed to be perfectly well. Yesterday lunchtime he looked feverish. Yegor, who of course noticed nothing, spoke of how he was missing the typewriter he had become so attached to, and hoped it would be coming back soon. To which Lyu said, 'Please don't say that! I would rather it was away a long while!' I once read about a famous actor who would occasionally get drunk before a performance and become so disorientated that one thought it impossible he would be able to act. But when it was time for him to step on stage he composed himself with demonic willpower and gave a spellbinding performance. Only seldom did this power wane slightly, allowing his true state to become evident. This is what Lyu reminded me of at that moment. He was permanently on the verge of delirium. I urgently put it to him that he had a fever and must go to bed. He admitted this too, but argued that in such circumstances it was better for him to keep moving, and wanted to go for a bicycle ride. Not to be dissuaded, he went off and came back three hours later, bathed in sweat and utterly worn out. Then he went to lie down without eating anything. Today he has stayed in bed, exhausted, but he really does seem to have broken his fever. The doctor, who came because of Ivan, admitted that such treatments can work some-times, although he'd never prescribe them as they are not suited to everyone. Lyu is an extraordinary man; he mesmerizes you time and again.

Dear Tatyana, I cannot wait for us to be alone! I like caring for patients, and it's so nice that I can do something for Lyu. It's really not much, for in fact one cannot care for him, he's a man who can only give; he lacks the organ for receiving. But I had been so look-ing forward to being alone with Yegor and all these unexpected occurrences seem like a malicious obstacle, insinuating itself between us and our longed-for days on our own. Velya and Jessika would have come to you today, but they did not wish to leave before it was clear whether Lyu was seriously ill or not. The danger has now passed, thank goodness! Just think how the feelings of love would have intensified in Jessika's soft heart! As soon as he can be moved, Ivan will be transferred to hospital, and until he has recovered a reliable man, who has often helped us out in the past, will stand in for him. I thought of coming into town with Yegor, to see the children off, but he says that he specifically took a holiday to go to the country for his health. He'd rather not be seen in Petersburg as it could be misconstrued. He also thinks that I'd be far more affected by their departure if we went there; I'd get terribly upset and start crying, et cetera. Indeed, I am bound to cry. They will surely be away for a year, if not longer, otherwise there's no point. A whole year without my two children! If I didn't have Yegor to myself at the moment! Well, I'm no longer so young that a year seems a long time; it's only twelve times thirty days – it's merely the twinkling of an eye! How happy I am that Peter is going too; I shall instruct the children to follow him.

Yours, Lusinya

VELYA TO KATYA

Kremskoye, 20th July

My little trumpet blast,

You can blare out to your heart's content, for tomorrow I leave. Go ahead and blare out your disapproval; it won't hurt as I shan't hear it and so it will be of no use to you. We can do no better deed for Papa and Mama at the moment than go away. A note has already appeared in the newspapers about the 'red university'. Nothing bad can happen to those involved except for, at most, the courses being suspended. But of course Father would rather we weren't here. The gaffer is still alive. Today he asked for a drop of schnapps, so it seems as if he is on the mend. As I cannot say goodbye to him because of the risk of infection, I wrote him a farewell poem. It begins:

> *Five times has the sun now sunk,*
> *Since the gaffer last got drunk.*

And finishes:

> *As I cannot kiss your loyal hand,*
> *Ere I leave for another land,*
> *I shall pray you soon find release:*
> *Either get well soon or rest in peace.*

I read it to Lyu, who is still in bed. He couldn't stop laughing, although he's really weak. He said he's convinced Ivan will think I'm Russia's greatest poet and that my verse is the epitome of all poetry. He envied people who could achieve emotional rapture through rhythm and simple rhyme alone. Lyu would like to come with us to Petersburg, but he fears he'll still be too weak and Mama will not let him go. So you will not see him again. With her love for him, Jessika is a silly little worm, but I advise you to treat her gently, my sweet sister, rather than scolding and pecking her. She is just like a dewdrop that in the sun shines as beautifully as a diamond and is bursting with life, but when the sun disappears loses its lustre and dries up. I am writing this so you see that I can express myself in proper poetry too. Tell Peter to acquire cigars and cigarettes for the journey; he likes being given tasks to accomplish.

Velya

LYU TO KONSTANTIN

Kremskoye, 23rd July

Dear Konstantin,

You refrained from writing so that, were I mortally ill or dead, the letter should not fall into the wrong hands. Now the danger is past. If you hear no more from me, have the typewriter sent off on the 31st and let me know immediately. My sickness has finally broken, but I am still very tired, so tired that I should wish to lie in bed a few days more, without thinking, without any other pictures in my mind than those of the dark woman and blonde girl who from time to time float through my room, bend over me and speak kindly with their soft voices, or those of the firs and birches I can see through my open window. Will there ever be a man who can gaze at beauty without torment, without the divine, execrable sting of the soul?

Tomorrow Velya and Jessika are travelling to Petersburg. Jessika will stay with her aunt. When I see her again she will be wearing a black dress. Last night, when I glimpsed the moon shining pallidly, surrounded by dark clouds, I could not but help think of her blonde head atop the black dress. Oh, that is the least of it. She will have rosy cheeks once more, and smile and wear white dresses. The fact that everything, by virtue of coming into existence, is doomed to pass – that is the sole tragedy of life, for it is the nature of life, for life so constructed is the only one that can ever be ours. I await your news.

Lyu

LUSINYA TO KATYA

24th July

My dear youngest,

Today Velya and Jessika are leaving. They waited one more day for Lyu, but ultimately dissuaded him from taking on the strain of travelling today. Although he got up, he's still weak. He'll certainly be spending around three more days here, so there's no way you will see him again if you leave the day after tomorrow. Jessika has been battling bravely with her feelings; I wouldn't have imagined her capable of such willpower. This morning she was up very early in the garden, filling baskets with roses that she decorated the entire house with. 'I think it's like a wedding house,' she said. Then she said, 'Mama, we must really have got in your way when we arrived so quickly one after the other.' I said, 'Yes, if we hadn't ourselves to blame, we might have been slightly annoyed.' Your brother Velya, who had come into the room, said to her, 'My God, what are you thinking? They'd have been bored to death without us.' An incensed Jessika: 'You arrogant boy! You're so lazy you didn't speak before you were two and didn't make a joke before you were ten.' Well, I'm sure you can imagine how daintily they yapped at one another. And then that little face, so quiet and pale beneath the old childish laughter. Give her lots of love on your last day, do you hear me, my sweet thing? And don't offend her by saying anything bad about Lyu. You are far too young and foolish a glow-worm to be able to judge him properly. In any case, he's a brilliant man and one must take care to think the best of brilliant people. In case of doubt, one ought to hold back with one's judgement.

As for the chauffeur that Aunt Tatyana suggests we engage instead of the old retainer, Papa cannot come to a decision, even though he admits that it would perhaps be more agreeable for us. He says he doesn't want to have a complete stranger in the house, as the revolution-ary party has regularly smuggled its people into houses to gather private information or communicate with the servants. He is unhappy at the prospect of introducing an uncertain element into the circle of our loyal and dependable servants. As Papa is free of any fearfulness, this caution is surely justified. So we'll stick with old Kyrill; he doesn't drink any more than Ivan, and Papa says that drunkards have the most loyal hearts.

An embrace from me, my beloved child! I send my love to all three of you and please promise me that you and Velya won't squabble on the journey. Don't call each other monkey or newt or birdbrain – the last of these is just about acceptable, if it must be – for jokes can become serious, and anyway it is a beastly habit which may shock people who don't know you. Please also keep an eye on Velya, as if you were the elder, but without letting him notice. I worry more about him than about you. I know you will do the right thing, my darling, and that something good will come of you.

So now I am a childless woman! But I have you all firmly in my heart; you're still small and like sitting close to your mama in a tiny room.

Farewell!

Velya and Katya to Yegor

Petersburg, 26th July

Dear Papa,

When Katya read your line in Mama's letter that drunkards have the most loyal hearts, she blurted out,

'You see? Lyu isn't a drinker! He only drank wine because of its beautiful colour and the aroma!' Now the rumour is certain to go around that you only released Lyu because he's never been drunk. You'll become a darling of the people and a horde of lurching Cossacks will permanently surround you as voluntary body-guards. Two evenings ago we persuaded Aunt Tatyana to serve us some really fine wine for our leaving dinner and Peter, who was just about to join a temperance association, has now deferred this until our return.

Dear Papa,

Velya is writing utter nonsense. It's impossible to live with him without shouting out monkey or newt. Mama, you ought to have brought him up better from the outset. You are absolutely right about the drinking, Papa; it was an absurd idea of Peter's to want to join a temperance association. Why shouldn't you drink if it's to your taste? How foolish! Jessika says we need not worry on your account; the two of you looked so young and happy. That's how we want to imagine you when we're away. I'm very nice to Jessika, but she's a silly goose. Here is our carriage arriving! Tomorrow at this time we shall already be over the border. On the way I shall write you a properly long letter, sweet Mama.

Katya

Lyu to Konstantin

Kremskoye, 1st August

Dear Konstantin,

I shall be leaving tomorrow morning. I am taking the motorcar to Petersburg. From there I shall drive to my father's. I assume that the typewriter is arriving this evening. I should not care for it to arrive earlier, because the governor would then probably demand to start writing. Like little children, the two of them are looking forward to being alone. They have no idea what actually awaits them – my God, what does one expect when one is anticipating a momentary surge of love? What does one find?

As far as I am concerned, it is out of the question that someone else could use the machine before the governor, the one thing that could ruin my plan. The maids are too scared of the governor to lay a finger on it, especially as it has already broken once. He has even forbidden them to dust the typewriter, saying he will do it himself. I am sure he will use it very soon; he always has a few letters to write and he will wish to try it out after the repair. It will be no longer than a day. I suspect he will write to the children. She – his wife – what will become of her? It would be best for her if she were at his side, as is almost always the case. The next time I come to Petersburg I should like to see you. But first I need some peace and quiet.

Lyu

LUSINYA TO JESSIKA

Kremskoye, 1st August

Jessika, my petal, your roses have now faded, even before our joy at being alone could begin. The garden, however, is full of new blooms. Lyu is leaving early tomorrow morning. He has already said his goodbyes, for he is setting off before we get up. Earlier, when we were returning from a walk, a man was standing at the garden door. I didn't notice him until we were quite close and I gave an involuntary start. Lyu laughed and said, 'It must be the delivery man again with the typewriter.' And indeed it was. I looked at him in both horror and admiration, and he laughed once more, with Papa joining in. It was only natural that he should guess correctly, as in fact we had been expecting the typewriter with the first post. Let me tell you that Papa didn't pounce immediately on the crate, but let Lyu unpack it. Now Papa is still sitting with me, playing the piano more beautifully than anyone else in the world. Perhaps at the same time the lime blossoms of your voice are fragrant beside Aunt Tatyana's piano. You know, don't you, that Lyu said your singing was so delicate one could not say it sounded, but rather gave off a sweet scent. At this moment I fancy I can hear you, my little lovely.

Lyu gave me another of his inscrutable looks when he said goodbye. I'm glad I shall not have to meet this gaze again tomorrow. But calm down: I gave him the most wonderful basket of food for the journey and wish him all the best. If he didn't sleepwalk I would be his friend without fail. Just imagine, the gaffer expressed his outrage that Lyu was leaving before he was back on his feet, for he was sick and frail and didn't count, and there must be a man in the house. At which Papa said, 'What am I? A stork?' Ivan wept at first, and then said he'd never regarded Papa as a stork, but he was supposed to be under protection at the moment and you couldn't protect yourself, just as you couldn't wash your own back. Papa asked Mariushka, who had reported this to us, 'Who washes his back then? You?' Which she indignantly denied, and so this remains a mystery.

Good night, darling. When will I decorate your hair with roses again? Who knows how soon? Beautiful things come unexpectedly overnight.

Yours, Mama

YEGOR TO VELYA AND KATYA

Kremskoye, 2nd August

Well, my two little children, what nonsense is that about drinking? What am I supposed to have said? Educated people must be moderate, that stands to reason. If a

Russian peasant does not drink, one can conclude that there is calculation involved, a desire for some sort of improvement, and where the animal drive is broken, nothing good takes its place at first. So, to be regarded as educated people, be moderate. Our guardian angel has left and for the time being I have no one here save for Mother, beneath whose wings I feel most comfortable. She is just approaching my chair, putting her arm around me and posing that question which is old hat now, but which I still love to hear: 'Why are you so pale, Y

Subscribe

Peirene Press publishes series of world-class contemporary novellas. An annual subscription consists of three books chosen from across the world connected by a single theme.

The books will be sent out in December (in time for Christmas), May and September. Any title in the series already in print when you order will be posted immediately.

The perfect way for book lovers to collect all the Peirene titles.

'A class act.' GUARDIAN

'Two-hour books to be devoured in a single sitting: literary cinema for those fatigued by film.' TLS

£35   1 Year Subscription (3 books, free p&p)

£65   2 Year Subscription (6 books, free p&p)

£90   3 Year Subscription (9 books, free p&p)

Peirene Press, 17 Cheverton Road, London N19 3BB
T 020 7686 1941
E subscriptions@peirenepress.com

www.peirenepress.com/shop
with secure online ordering facility

Peirene's Series

FEMALE VOICE: INNER REALITIES

....

MALE DILEMMA: QUESTS FOR INTIMACY

SMALL EPIC: UNRAVELLING SECRETS

NO 7
The Brothers by Asko Sahlberg
Translated from the Finnish by Emily Jeremiah and Fleur Jeremiah
'Intensely visual.' INDEPENDENT ON SUNDAY

NO 8
The Murder of Halland by Pia Juul
Translated from the Danish by Martin Aitken
'A brilliantly drawn character.' TLS

NO 9
Sea of Ink by Richard Weihe
Translated from the Swiss German by Jamie Bulloch
'Delicate and moving.' INDEPENDENT

....
TURNING POINT: REVOLUTIONARY MOMENTS

NO 10
The Mussel Feast by Birgit Vanderbeke
Translated from the German by Jamie Bulloch
'An extraordinary book.' STANDPOINT

NO 11
Mr Darwin's Gardener by Kristina Carlson
Translated from the Finnish by Emily Jeremiah and Fleur Jeremiah
'Something miraculous.' GUARDIAN

NO 12
Chasing the King of Hearts by Hanna Krall
Translated from the Polish by Philip Boehm
'A remarkable find.' SUNDAY TIMES

COMING-OF-AGE: TOWARDS IDENTITY

NO 13
The Dead Lake by Hamid Ismailov
Translated from the Russian by Andrew Bromfield
'Immense poetic power.' GUARDIAN

NO 14
The Blue Room by Hanne Ørstavik
Translated from the Norwegian by Deborah Dawkin
'Shrewd and psychologically adroit.' LANCASHIRE
EVENING POST

NO 15
Under the Tripoli Sky by Kamal Ben Hameda
Translated from the French by Adriana Hunter
'It is excellent.' SUNDAY TIMES

....
CHANCE ENCOUNTER: MEETING THE OTHER

NO 16
White Hunger by Aki Ollikainen
Translated from the Finnish by Emily Jeremiah and Fleur Jeremiah
'A tale of epic substance.' LOS ANGELES REVIEW OF BOOKS

NO 17
Reader for Hire by Raymond Jean
Translated from the French by Adriana Hunter
'A book that will make you want to read more books.'
COSMOPOLITAN

NO 18
The Looking-Glass Sisters by Gøhril Gabrielsen
Translated from the Norwegian by John Irons
*'The real strength of this book lies in the way so much
is withheld.'* DAILY MAIL

FAIRY TALE: END OF INNOCENCE

....
NEW IN 2016
EAST AND WEST: LOOKING BOTH WAYS

COUNTERPOINTS ARTS

Peirene Press is proud to support
Counterpoints Arts.

Counterpoints Arts is a charity that promotes the
creative arts by and about refugees and migrants
in the UK.

---

*'We are living in a time of human
displacement. We need bold and
imaginative interventions to help
us make sense of migration. And
who better to do this than artists
who are engaging with this issue.'*

ALMIR KOLDZIC AND ÁINE O'BRIEN, DIRECTORS, COUNTERPOINTS ARTS

By buying this book you are helping
Counterpoints Arts enhance the cultural
integration of refugees – a mission which will
surely change our society for the better.

Peirene will donate 50p from the sale of this
book to the charity.

www.counterpointsarts.org.uk